A SWEET
LITTLE MAID

AMY E. BLANCHARD

1st WORLD
LIBRARY
Literary Society

A Sweet Little Maid

Amy E. Blanchard

© 1st World Library, 2006
PO Box 2211
Fairfield, IA 52556
www.1stworldlibrary.com
First Edition

LCCN: 2006936186

Softcover ISBN: 978-1-4218-3021-6
Hardcover ISBN: 978-1-4218-2921-0
eBook ISBN: 978-1-4218-3121-3

Purchase *"A Sweet Little Maid"*
as a traditional bound book at:
www.1stWorldLibrary.com/purchase.asp?ISBN=978-1-4218-3021-6

1st World Library is a literary, educational organization
dedicated to:

- Creating a free internet library of downloadable ebooks

- Hosting writing competitions and offering book
  publishing scholarships.

Interested in more 1st World Library books?
contact: literacy@1stworldlibrary.com
Check us out at: www.1stworldlibrary.com

1ˢᵗ World Library Literary Society

Giving Back to the World

"If you want to work on the core problem, it's early school literacy."

- James Barksdale, former CEO of Netscape

"No skill is more crucial to the future of a child, or to a democratic and prosperous society, than literacy."

- Los Angeles Times

Literacy... means far more than learning how to read and write... The aim is to transmit... knowledge and promote social participation."

- UNESCO

"Literacy is not a luxury, it is a right and a responsibility. If our world is to meet the challenges of the twenty-first century we must harness the energy and creativity of all our citizens."

- President Bill Clinton

"Parents should be encouraged to read to their children, and teachers should be equipped with all available techniques for teaching literacy, so the varying needs and capacities of individual kids can be taken into account."

- Hugh Mackay

CONTENTS

CHAPTER I

DIMPLE AND BUBBLES

"Is yuh asleep, Miss Dimple?"

"No," said Dimple, drowsily.

"I'm are."

"Why, Bubbles," replied Dimple, "if you were asleep you wouldn't be talking."

"Folks talks in their sleep sometimes, Miss Dimple," answered Bubbles, opening her black eyes.

"Well, maybe they do, but your eyes are open now."

"I have herd of people sleepin' with their eyes open," returned Bubbles, nothing abashed.

"O, Bubbles, I don't believe it; for that is how to go to sleep; mamma says, 'shut your eyes and go to sleep,' she never says, 'open your eyes and go to sleep;' so there!"

Bubbles sat thoughtfully looking at her toes, having nothing to say when Dimple brought her mamma into the question.

"I'll tell you what, Bubbles," said Dimple, after a moment's pause, rising from the long grass where the two had been sitting. "Let's play Indian. You make such a lovely Indian, just like a real one. I am almost afraid of you when you are painted up, and have feathers in your head."

Bubbles grinned at the compliment.

"I will be the white maiden to be captured," said Dimple, as Bubbles coolly proceeded to take off her frock, displaying a red flannel petticoat.

"I'll hunt up the feathers, and you get ready," Dimple went on. "And the shawl—we must have the striped shawl for a blanket," and, running into the house, she soon came out with a little striped shawl, and a handful of stiff feathers. The shawl was arranged over Bubbles' shoulders, and produced a fine effect, when the feathers were stuck in her head.

"Now if you could only have the hatchet. You go get it, Bubbles."

"I dassent," said Bubbles.

"Oh yes, you dare," Dimple said, coaxingly. "I'd go ask mamma, but it is so hot and I've been in the house once."

"Deed, Miss Dimple"—Bubbles began.

"Don't you 'deed me. I tell you to go and I mean it. I'll send you to the orphan asylum, if you don't, and I wonder how you will like that; no more cakes, no more chicken and corn-bread for you, Miss Bubbles. Mush and milk, miss."

This dreadful threat had its desired effect, and Bubbles' bare black legs went scudding through the grass, and were back in a twinkling.

"Hyah it is," she said. "I was skeered, sho' 'nough."

"Oh well, you are a goose," said Dimple. "Who ever heard of

Amy E. Blanchard

an Indian being scared at a hatchet? Now I will go into the woodshed—that is my house, you know—and you must skulk softly along, and when you get to the door bang it open with the hatchet, and give a whoop."

So Dimple went in her house and shut the door, fearfully peeping through the cracks once in a while, as the terrible foe crept softly nearer and nearer, then with a terrific yell burst in.

"Please, Mr. Indian, don't scalp me."

"Ugh!" said the Indian.

"What shall I do?" said Dimple. "Make me take off my stockings and shoes, Bubbles. You know the captives must go barefooted."

"Ugh!" said the Indian, pointing to Dimple's feet.

"My shoes and stockings? Well, I will give them to you," and she quickly took them off. The Indian gravely tied them around his neck, and taking Dimple by the hand he led her forth in triumph.

But here a disaster followed, for the captive, thinking it her duty to struggle, knocked the hatchet out of the Indian's hand, and it fell with its edge on Dimple's little white foot, making a bad gash.

"Oh, you've killed me, sure enough," she cried. "Oh, you wicked, wicked thing!"

Poor Bubbles cried quite as hard as she, and begged not to be sent to the orphan asylum.

"Oh! your mother will whip me," she cried. "I 'spect I ought to be killed, but 'deed I didn't mean to, Miss Dimple; I wisht it had been my old black foot."

"I wish it had," sobbed Dimple. "Oh, I am bleeding all to nothing! Take me to mamma, Bubbles!"

Bubbles stooped down and, being a little larger and stronger, managed to carry her to the house.

Dimple's mamma was horrified when they appeared at her door. Bubbles in war-paint and feathers, carrying the little barefooted girl, from whose foot blood was dropping on the floor.

"What on earth is the matter? Oh, Dimple! Oh, Bubbles! What have you been doing?"

But Bubbles was so overcome by terror, and Dimples by the sight of the blood, that neither could explain till the foot was washed and bandaged.

Then poor Bubbles flung herself on the floor and begged not to be sent to the orphan asylum.

"You ridiculous child," said Dimple's mamma. "Of course you ought to be careful, but it is not your fault any more than Dimple's. She should not have sent you for the hatchet. I am very sorry for my little Dimple; it is not so very serious, but she will not be able to walk for several days. Next time you want to play Indian, do without a hatchet. Put on your frock, Bubbles, and go into the kitchen, for I'm sure I heard Sylvy call you."

Bubbles went meekly out and Dimple was soon asleep on the sofa.

Bubbles' real name was Barbara. She was the child of a former servant who went away, leaving her, when she was about five years old, with Mrs. Dallas; as the mother never came back, and no one could tell of her whereabouts, Bubbles gradually became a fixture in Dimple's home.

Dimple, when she was just beginning to talk, tried hard to say

Amy E. Blanchard

Barbara, but got no nearer to it than Bubbles, and Bubbles the little darkey was always called.

Dimple herself was called so from the deep dimple in one cheek. Every one knew her by her pet name, and most persons forgot that her name ever was Eleanor.

She and Bubbles were devoted comrades. Bubbles would cheerfully have let Dimple walk over her and never forgot to call her *Miss* Dimple, thereby expressing her willingness to serve her.

Dimple was the dearest little girl in the world, but considering Bubbles her special property, made her do pretty much as she pleased, and her most dreadful threat was to send her to the orphan asylum.

She had once said, "Mamma, if you hadn't let Bubbles stay here, where would you have sent her?"

"To the orphan asylum, I suppose," her mamma answered; and Bubbles, hearing it, was ever after in mortal terror of the place, for Dimple gave her a graphic description of it, telling her she would never have anything to eat but mush and milk.

Dimple's foot did not get well as fast as she expected, and the little girl found it rather tiresome to lie on a lounge all day, although her mamma read to her, and tried to amuse her. Bubbles, too, was as obedient a nurse as could be, and, because she had been the cause of the accident, considered it her first and only duty to wait on Dimple.

"Mamma," said Dimple, "for a colored girl, Bubbles is the nicest I ever saw; but indeed, I should like a white girl to play with, just for a change. Couldn't you get me one?"

"Perhaps so," said her mamma. "We will see what can be done."

"Good-bye, little girl," said her papa the next morning. "I am going away and will not be back till to-morrow. What shall I bring you? A new doll?"

"Oh, please, papa; and papa a white girl if you can get one that is real nice, something the same kind of girl that I am."

"A girl like you would be hard to find, I think," said he, laughing, "but I'll inquire around and see if there is one to be had."

Bubbles looked very sober all day, and rolled her eyes around at Dimple in such a reproachful way that finally she said:

"I know just what you think, Bubbles. You believe I am going to send you to the orphan asylum and get a white girl, but I am not at all. If I get a white girl I shall want you all the same, because you will have to wait on her too."

Bubbles' face lighted up, as she said,

"Deed, cross my heart, Miss Dimple, I didn't fo' sure think yuh was gwine to send me off, but I tuck and thought yuh was conjurin' up somethin' agin me."

"Why, Bubbles, I wouldn't do such a thing, unless you were out and out bad. It has been such a long day," she said, turning to her mamma. "When will it be to-morrow?"

Mrs. Dallas drew up a little table, and Bubbles brought Dimple's best set of dishes, and with a clean cloth spread on first, the dishes were arranged. Then Bubbles brought in a little dish of chicken, a glass of jelly, light rolls, little cakes, a pitcher of milk, tea, sugar, and butter; and then Mrs. Dallas said,

"We will have our supper together, because papa is away, and Bubbles can wait on us here."

Bubbles had disappeared, but presently came back with a

bunch of roses, which she put in the middle of the table.

"Why, Bubbles, that is quite fine," said Dimple, and she ate her supper with a relish; after which, the time seemed very short until to-morrow, for she was soon asleep.

"I believe this day is long too," she said, toward the afternoon of the next day. "When will papa come?"

"Not till six o'clock," replied her mamma. "You must try to be patient, for I think you will be very glad when he gets here. I have sent Bubbles for a book, and I will read to you, to pass the time away."

Six o'clock came at last, and soon after Dimple heard her papa's voice in the hall.

"Come right up," she heard him say.

"I do believe he has brought the white girl," she said, clasping her hands; and, to be sure, when he opened the door, some one was behind him.

"This is the nearest like you I could get," he said, and led forward some one in a grey frock and hat.

Dimple screamed, "Why, it is Florence. Oh! papa, you didn't say you were going to auntie's!"

"No. I wanted to surprise you," he replied. "And I thought your own cousin ought to be more like you than any one else."

"Well, I am delighted. You are sure to stay a long, long time, Florence. Take off your hat and sit right here," she said, moving up on the lounge. "I never had such a surprise."

"You forgot I promised a doll, too," said her papa, as he opened a package. "I thought Florence would like one, so I brought two, as near alike as if they were cousins," he added.

"Oh! you preciousest papa," said Dimple; "let me hug you all to pieces. I do think you are the most delightful man. I don't wonder mamma married you. When you go down please send Bubbles up here, so I can tell her I am almost glad she cut my foot, for it is worth it, to have Florence and a new doll too."

Bubbles came in beaming.

"Bubbles," cried Dimple, "see Florence and our new dolls, —and Bubbles, you shall have one of my old ones,—and Bubbles, when I grow up, you shall live with me always, because you cut my foot, and you must never, never think of the orphan asylum again.

"Now, tell me, Florence," she said, turning to her, "all about your coming. Didn't you have to get ready in a hurry?"

"Yes, indeed," replied Florence, "and, oh Dimple, I was so glad when uncle asked mamma and she said 'yes,' and she just packed up my things in a jiffy, and we stopped at papa's office, and said good-bye to him, and uncle bought me oranges and papers on the cars, and we didn't seem a bit long coming."

"Well, I am too glad," returned Dimple. "Won't we have fun with the dolls? O, Florence, do eat your supper up here with me instead of going downstairs."

"Of course," said Florence, "unless you would rather go down, for uncle said he would carry you."

"I know," said Dimple, "but it is more fun to have it up here with my tea-set, and Bubbles to wait on us."

So they had their tea upstairs, with the table set by the window, where the wistaria peeped in to look at them, and a little brown bird, quite envious, put his head on one side, and stood on the sill a full minute before he flew away.

"Oh! I think it is just lovely here," said Florence. "Ever so

Amy E. Blanchard

much nicer than at our house."

"Do you think so?" said Dimple, quite pleased. "You have a lovely house, though, Florence; it is four stories high, and has such beautiful things in it, and when you look out of the windows there is so much to see, carriages, and people all dressed up."

"Yes, and dirty old beggars and ragmen," said Florence, "and nasty, muddy streets."

They both laughed.

"What cunning little doylies," said Florence. "Who worked the little figures on them?"

"Mamma," said Dimple. "Aren't they sweet? She always sends them up with my supper, one over the milk pitcher, and one over the cake. Do you like lots of sugar in your tea, Florence?"

"Two lumps."

"Only two! Why I like three, and I believe I could take another; mamma says I have a sweet tooth, but I don't know where it is, for I have put my tongue on all of them and they all taste alike. Bubbles, go down and ask mamma if we mayn't have a little teensy-weensy bit more honey, we are both so hungry."

Bubbles took the little glass dish, and went off.

"I wish I had a Bubbles," said Florence. "We have a black man, but I think a little girl is ever so much nicer; then there is nurse, she takes us to walk; and then there is Kate, the cook, and Lena, the chambermaid, they are always fussing and quarreling. I get tired of so many."

"We only have Sylvy and Bubbles," said Dimple. "Sylvy is black too; she is real nice but she will get mad with Bubbles sometimes. Bubbles cleans knives, and runs errands, sets the table, wipes the dishes, and is a lot of help. You don't know how much she can do, and she learns something new every little while. Have some more honey, Florence, for that piece of bread. I never can come out even; sometimes I have to take more bread for the honey, and then more honey for the bread, till I do eat so much. Have you finished? I believe I have too."

"It is *so* nice here," said Florence, as they settled themselves after their tea, "just delicious. It is so much pleasanter to see green grass, and trees, and flowers, than brick walls, and pavements. Do you play out of doors much?"

"Yes, all day, nearly; but I haven't since my foot was hurt. I couldn't run about, and I should have to wait for some one to bring me in; then I always want to be close to mamma when anything is the matter with me. Are you that way?"

"Yes," said Florence. "Aren't mammas the best thing in the world? I hope mine doesn't miss me."

"Now, Florence, don't get homesick, for I shall be distressed if you do. Let's talk about the dolls. Here comes mamma. We will ask her what we can dress them in.

"Mamma, mamma, did you see our beauty dolls? Won't you get out your reserve bag to-morrow? I have looked over my piece box so much, and it would be perfectly splendid to have something I had never seen before."

"What is a reserve bag?" asked Florence.

"Why, you see," said Dimple, "mamma has a lot of bags, one for silk pieces, and one for white pieces, and one for pieces like our frocks, and so on, but the nicest is the one she keeps for occasions, like Christmas and birthdays and fairs, and there are the prettiest bits of velvet and silk in it. Mamma, bring out your reserve bag, that is a lovely blue-eyed mamma," said Dimple, coaxingly.

Amy E. Blanchard

"You are very complimentary," said her mamma, laughing. "If you won't tease or worry me, to-morrow I will bring it out and you can each choose what you want."

"Oh! mamma, you are lovelier and more blue-eyed than ever," said Dimple, "let us both kiss you. We will be good as gold, won't we, Florence?"

"Yes, indeed," said she. "Auntie, you are lovely."

"I think if you don't go to bed," said Mrs. Dallas, "you will keep me awake all night with your flattery."

"Florence is to sleep with me, isn't she, mamma?"

"Certainly, and the sooner you go, the sooner it will be to-morrow."

"Well, we will go now. See me ride, Florence," said Dimple, as her mamma put her in a rocking-chair and pushed the chair along through the door into Dimple's little blue and white room.

It was a dear little room, and Dimple, with the help of Bubbles, took care of it all herself.

There was a white curtained window around which roses and honeysuckle grew, and threw their tendrils about in a such a reckless way, that one or two had made up their minds to live in the room instead of outdoors, and were climbing around the window sash.

A little brass bedstead, a mantel with a blue and white lambrequin, a blue and white toilet set, pretty pictures on the wall, and a small bookshelf, made a very cozy looking nest for a little girl, and so Florence thought, who had no room of her own, but slept with an older sister.

They were both tired, and even the delightful topic of dolls could not keep them awake very long, for a half hour later when the moon looked in on her way across the sky, she saw them both sound asleep, an auburn head on Florence's pillow, and a yellow one on Dimple's.

Amy E. Blanchard

CHAPTER II

DOLLS

Florence and Dimple were on the back porch where it was always cool in the morning.

Bubbles was cleaning knives on the steps, the temptation to watch the dressing of the dolls being too great to keep her in the kitchen.

"I declare," said Dimple, "we haven't named them yet."

"That is so," returned Florence.

"You take first choice, then," said Dimple. "I shall have to think, for I've had a Rose and a Violet and a Lily, besides one named Victoria, and one Aurelia."

Florence sat still watching Bubbles briskly scouring her knives. "Dear me," she said, presently, "it's awfully hard. How do you suppose our mothers found names for us?"

"Oh! that was easy enough," answered Dimple. "I was named Eleanor after your mamma, and you were named Florence after mine; but, you see we are not sisters, so we can't do that. I'll tell you what let's do; you tell mamma the names you like best, and I will tell her those I like; then she can write them down and put them in a hat, and we will draw lots for them."

"That will be a good plan," said Florence. "She is coming now with the reserve bag."

"Oh! Oh! Oh!" they cried, as Mrs. Dallas shook out its contents.

"Let Florence choose first, dear," said she as Dimple began making dives at the fluttering ends of silk. "You may each have two pieces."

Dimple looked a little disappointed; being an only child she was used to first choice herself, but she yielded with a very good grace.

Florence finally chose a piece of maroon satin, and another of yellow brocaded velvet, while Dimple picked out a piece of silk with velvet stripes of a lovely pink, and another bit of blue silk brocade. "Mamma," whispered she, "give Bubbles a little piece, if she is black," and so the brightest bit of scarlet was picked out for Bubbles, who was made perfectly happy by it.

"Now, names," exclaimed Dimple, as the rest of the pieces were returned to the bag. "First Florence one and then I one. How many, Florence?"

"Four, I think. Ethel first, for me. No, you choose first, Dimple. I had first choice in the pieces."

"No, you're company."

Being company, Florence took her rights, and Ethel went down.

"Blanche, for me, mamma," said Dimple.

"And Celestine for me, auntie."

"Irene," said Dimple.

"Geraldine," said Florence.

"Adele," said Dimple.

"My last," said Florence. "Rubina."

"Oh, what a lovely name!" exclaimed Dimple. "If you don't draw it, I should like it, so I won't say any more till you have drawn."

The slips were shaken up in a hat, and Florence, with eyes shut, drew out Celestine.

"I am glad," she said. "I believe I like that best; it has a sort of a heavenly sound, and my doll is angelic."

"Well, mamma, I will take Rubina. You don't care, do you, Florence?"

"No, indeed. I am glad you like it."

"Now they are named, we will dress them."

"How are you going to dress yours, Dimple?"

"I think I'll have a skirt of the blue and a waist of the pink. No, the other way, will look best, because the velvet is thickest, the skirt of pink and the waist of blue."

"Well, I will have to make my doll's frock of all the same, with velvet trimming. Will that look well?"

"Lovely! What are you going to do with your piece, Bubbles?"

"Make a overskirt for Floridy Alabamy," said Bubbles, importantly.

"Who?" said Dimple, with her scissors ready to cut into the pink.

"Floridy Alabamy," said Bubbles, gravely.

"What a name!" shrieked Dimple, throwing back her head in a fit of laughter. "Florence, *did* you hear? Floridy Alabamy."

And the girls laughed till the tears ran down their cheeks.

"Bubbles, you are too ridiculous," said Dimple, while Bubbles pinned her bit of scarlet on her doll.

Just then Sylvy called her, and she ran off, holding her doll admiringly at arm's length.

"She will dress it just like a darkey. You see," said Dimple, "she has a purple dress on it now; think of that, with a scarlet overskirt; and I know she will make it a blue waist out of one of my old sash ribbons I gave her."

And sure enough, Floridy Alabamy did wear the three colors in triumph.

"Do you like big or little dolls best?" asked Florence.

"I don't know," said Dimple. "I think rather big or real little. Middle sizes are so hard to dress. They have to have such little fidgety sleeves and waists. I have two little dolls upstairs, and we can dress them up next. I believe one of them has an arm off, but it can be mended. How many dolls have you?"

"Four, now," answered Florence. "I had five, but Gertrude broke one. Gertrude is such a mischief, I have to keep all my things locked up. I hope to goodness they won't let her get at them while I'm away."

"Oh, you must make a traveling dress for your Celestine. I have a piece of grey linen that will just do."

By the time the dinner bell rang, both the dolls were dressed gorgeously.

Amy E. Blanchard

"Aren't they lovely, papa?" said Dimple, as she hobbled out to meet him.

"Yes; they look like two butterflies," he said, lifting her up, doll and all.

"Are you having a good time, Florence? I hope Dimple hasn't pinched or scratched you yet."

"Why, papa," said Dimple, looking very much hurt. "Florence will think I am a regular little cat," but seeing a twinkle in his eyes, she knew he was only in fun, and was consoled by the kiss he gave her as he put her in her chair at the table.

There was a long afternoon before them, and, although Dimple could not walk very well with her bandaged foot, she managed to get down to her favorite place, under a big tree, where the grass was long and thick.

"Now we can play beautifully with our dolls, Florence," she said, "and have no one to disturb us, for Bubbles doesn't count. She has to be in the kitchen for a while anyhow."

They had not been out very long before Bubbles came running to them. "There is a lady and a boy in the house, Miss Dimple," she said, "and your mamma's a bringin' the boy out hyah."

"A boy!" said both the girls in horror.

"Think of it, Florence, a horrid boy! What will we do with him? I can't run, and boys despise dolls. As for talking, I never could talk to boys. They shut me up like a clam. I always feel as if they wanted to get away, and I believe they would if they could," said Dimple in a disgusted tone.

But, by this time, Mrs. Dallas had come up to them.

"This is Rock Hardy, girls," said she. "As Dimple is a little lame, I brought him out here, rather than take her in the house," and so saying, she left them. There was a deep silence after they had shaken hands; all looking rather bashful for a few minutes.

Finally Rock took courage to say, "What pretty dolls."

This was encouraging; Florence and Dimple exchanged pleased glances.

"Do you think they are pretty?" asked Dimple. "I thought boys hated dolls."

"I don't," said Rock. "I played with them myself for a long time, and I have one now, but I don't play with it because I like to read better."

"He *is* a nice boy," thought the girls.

"How funny," said Florence. "How came you to play with dolls?"

"Why, you see, I haven't any brothers and sisters. When I was a little fellow I used to get so lonely, that my mother dressed a boy doll for me, and I talked to it and pretended it was another boy."

"I haven't any brothers, or sisters either," said Dimple, "but Florence has. I have Bubbles, though. Everybody can't have a Bubbles; she is next best to a sister, or a cousin."

"Who is Bubbles?" asked Rock.

"She is the little colored girl you saw when you came out of the house; she has lived here ever since I was a baby; she is a year older than I am; her mother ran off and left her, and she is real nice to play with."

Dimple was fast getting over her embarrassment.

Amy E. Blanchard

"Don't you go to school?" asked Rock.

"No, mamma has always taught me at home, but I am going next year. It is vacation now."

"Yes, I know," said Rock, "that is why we came here. We are going to stay for some time. I like to play with girls. Will you let me come and play with you sometimes?"

"Yes, indeed," said Dimple, in her warm-hearted way. "My foot is nearly well, and I can soon run about. I think I should like to play with a nice boy."

"I hope I'm a nice boy," said Rock, "but I don't know. I suppose everybody is mean sometimes."

"I think you look nice," said Dimple, honestly, looking at him from head to foot.

"Why don't you say something, Florence?"

Florence thus appealed to, could say nothing.

"Florence is my cousin," said Dimple. "She lives in Baltimore and she came here yesterday."

"Why, I live in Baltimore," said Rock. "What street do you live on, Florence?"

Florence told him, and they found it was in the next street to that on which Rock lived, so they all began to feel like old friends.

"If I had my scroll saw here, I could make you each a chair for your dolls," said Rock. "Maybe my mother will let me send for it. I will ask her."

"Oh, that would be lovely," said the girls.

"And I will lend you some of my books to read," said Dimple. "If you will please hand me that little cane, we will go in and you can choose them."

"Oh, thank you," said Rock. "I shall like to have them, for I like to read better than to do anything else."

They all went in and found Rock's mother and Mrs. Dallas in the parlor.

Dimple told her mamma what they had come for, and her mamma suggested her taking Rock into the library first, as he might find something there that he liked.

So Rock was taken to the bookcase, and found there a book of travels he had been wanting to read, so he bade them good-bye, with it under his arm, promising soon to come again.

Then Dimple and Florence returned to the garden where they had left a colony of grasshoppers imprisoned in a small house built for them out of bits of wood and bark.

"Baby Grasshopper has gone," said Florence, in dismay, as she peeped in to see the prisoners.

"I knew he would get out; he was so little," returned Dimple. "Let's set them all free, Florence. We'll pretend that they escaped in the night, or that peace has been declared."

"Or that a tornado blew down their prison."

"Yes, that will be the best. We'll blow real hard, and maybe it will come down."

So, with cheeks much puffed out they blew and blew, but without avail, and finally they picked up their hats and fanned the little bark structure so vigorously that it toppled over, and the grasshoppers escaped in every direction, the children laughing to see how quickly they disappeared.

Amy E. Blanchard

They sat there in the grass wondering what to do next when Dimple exclaimed, "There comes papa with Mr. Coulter, —he's the carpenter, you know—I wonder what he is going to do. See, Mr. Coulter is measuring the ground, and papa is explaining something. I can tell by the way he keeps doing so, with his hand. He always does that when he is explaining. Help me up, Florence, and let's go over there and see what's going on. Papa must mean to have something built. I hope it isn't a fence. No, it can't be that, for it would be too near the other one. Isn't it funny to watch men talking? They do so many funny things. Mr. Coulter keeps nodding his head like a horse."

Florence laughed and they made their way over to where the two men stood. As soon as they were within speaking distance, Dimple began to put her questions. "Are you going to build something, papa? What is it? Please don't say it's a fence, or a—a pig-sty."

Mr. Coulter chuckled as he went on laying his foot-rule along the ground.

"I hope it won't turn into a pig-sty," Mr. Dallas replied, with a smile. "It won't unless little pigs get into it."

"Are you going to keep little pigs?" Dimple asked.

"I didn't say so."

"Oh, papa, you are so mystiferious. I wish you would tell us all about it. What are you going to build? Any sort of house?"

"Yes, one sort of house."

"What is it to be for?"

"Little chicks."

"Ah!" Dimple was quite satisfied. "I see. You need a new hen house. Isn't the old one big enough? To be sure we don't get very many eggs just now, for so many of the hens are sitting. Oh, I know, maybe you are going to build a place like Mr. Lind's, with a—what is that thing? A inkybator. Are you going to have one of those? and a brooder? Are you, papa?"

"I haven't decided exactly what is to be in it, just yet. I think we'll let mamma see to that—she knows best what is needed. You shall know all about it in good time. But, Dimple, I don't want you to worry Mr. Coulter with questions, and I want you two little girls to keep away from the building while the work is going on."

"Yes, uncle." Florence gave her promise promptly.

"Yes—papa—but—" Dimple was disappointed. She dearly liked to watch the workmen when they came on the place, and she felt this was a deprivation which seemed unnecessary. "Why, papa, can't we look at the workmen? We won't ask questions and bother them," she said.

"I think it is best that you shouldn't this time. Can't you trust papa? When the proper time comes I'll show you the whole thing, and explain it all. Meantime I want you to be an obedient little girl, and keep out of the way."

Dimple looked up wistfully.

"Won't you please your father by minding what he says?" continued Mr. Dallas.

"Yes, papa," replied Dimple, faintly, "I will be sure to mind, only I wish you could let me see the house going up. It is such fun to climb about over the boards and things."

"I know it is, and I know I'm requiring a great deal of you, but I think in the end you will see why," returned her father.

"Have we many little chicks to go in it. I mean will there be a

Amy E. Blanchard

great many?"

Mr. Dallas and Mr. Coulter glanced at each other and smiled; then Mr. Dallas said, "It might be a good plan to go to the barn and see how old Speckle is getting on. Her time is about up, so perhaps we'll find some little chicks. I'll carry you there on my back."

"And maybe we'll find some eggs," spoke up Florence, who dearly liked to hunt eggs. "We found two yesterday. Indeed, uncle, I think you do need more hens, for auntie said yesterday that she didn't get all the eggs she wanted."

They found old Speckle ready to be quite flustered when they took her off the nest, for they found that four little chicks were already hatched, and the shells of several other eggs were chipped.

Mr. Dallas gave the children each two of the little chicks to carry up to the house, that they might be kept safely till Speckle came off with the rest of the brood, and Bubbles, who had followed them, trotted along behind with her hands full of the eggs they were fortunate enough to find.

The new building was begun at once, and Dimple found it hard to keep away from it, but she resolutely stuck to her promise. One day, to be sure, she did not venture nearer than usual, but suddenly she exclaimed in a loud voice, "Get thee hence, satan!" and turning ran directly into Bubbles who, as usual, had followed her.

"What dat yuh call me, Miss Dimple," exclaimed Bubbles, in an aggrieved tone.

"You! Oh, I wasn't talking to you."

This seemed rather a lame excuse to Bubbles, since no one else was near. "Yass 'm, yuh is call me sumpin'," she insisted. "Dey ain't nobody else."

"There was somebody else," Dimple replied, with dignity. "And don't you contradict me. I reckon I know what I'm talking about better than you do."

This puzzled Bubbles, but it also silenced her, although she looked furtively around to see where Dimple's hidden acquaintance might be; that somebody else to whom she spoke so defiantly. "Hit's dat no 'count little niggah Jim, I'll be bound," she muttered, under her breath. "He done shy a stone at the de birds and dat mek Miss Dimple mad. She don't 'low nobody 'buse de birds." Thus settling the matter, she cheerfully smiled when Dimple gave her a glance, and Dimple laughed. Then she stood still.

"Bubbles," she said, "papa never said you mustn't go near that house, did he?"

"No 'm."

"Well, just go peep in and tell me what it looks like. From the looks of the outside, I should say that it is nearly done. You peep in at the window."

Bubbles obeyed, and came back with the information. "Hit's got a flo' an' a stove."

"Ah!" Dimple pondered. "Oh yes, that's to keep the baby chicks warm, I suppose. I wish I could see for myself. Is that all, Bubbles?"

"Yass 'm."

"I wish I hadn't told you to peep in," Dimple remarked, after a pause. "I don't believe it was quite honest for me to do it, and I'll have to be uncomfortable till I tell mamma or papa. You oughtn't to have peeped, Bubbles."

"Yuh tole me to."

"So I did, but—well, you shouldn't have done it, just the same."

Bubbles rolled her eyes reproachfully, and began to mutter.

"There, never mind. It wasn't your fault," Dimple confessed, hastily. But although Bubbles' countenance cleared, Dimple herself did not feel at ease till she had told her mother, which she did that night at bedtime.

"It was not right," her mother told her, "and was a bad example to Bubbles. That is where the trouble often comes in. Not so much in the actual wrong we do, but its effect upon others."

"I do want to see, so very much. Papa never made it so hard for me before."

"I know it, dear. I have realized very clearly all along how hard it must be for you, but I think when you do know you will be so pleased that you will forget this part of it. I am glad my little girlie was brave enough to tell of her asking Bubbles to peep."

And kissing her good-night, Mrs. Dallas left her little girl feeling comforted.

CHAPTER III

A QUARREL

"Raining! Isn't that too bad?" said Florence, leaning on one elbow in bed, and looking out of the window.

"Hm, hm," said Dimple, sleepily, from her pillow.

Florence slipped out of bed and stood looking dolefully at the falling drops.

"What do you suppose the birds do, Dimple?" she asked, going up to her, and softly shaking her.

"Oh," said Dimple, now awake, and sitting up in bed, rubbing her eyes, "I suppose they get under the leaves just as we do under an umbrella, or they go under the eaves, and places like that. I have seen them lots of times. It is raining, isn't it, Florence?"

"I said so, long ago," answered Florence; "now we can't go out of doors to play, and it is so nice outdoors. I don't see the sense of its raining in summer."

"Why," returned Dimple, sitting down on the floor to put on her shoes and stockings, "that is the very time for it to rain, or everything would dry up."

"Well, I wish it didn't have to," said Florence, coming away from the window, and sitting on the floor too. "What color stockings do you like best, Dimple?"

"I don't know; black, I think. Don't you?"

"I believe I do. My! there is the breakfast bell, and we are only beginning to get dressed. You fasten my buttons, and I will fasten yours, Dimple, so we will get dressed in a hurry."

Their fingers flew, and they rushed down to breakfast two steps at a time.

"It was so dark this morning that we went to sleep again after you called us, mamma," explained Dimple.

"I will excuse you this time, but your breakfast is not as warm as it would have been earlier," said Mrs. Dallas, "and papa had to go away without his morning kiss."

"I am sorry," said Dimple. "Cold eggs aren't very good," she went on, pushing away her plate. "What can we do to-day, mamma?"

"What should you like to do?"

"I don't know," returned Dimple. "My feelings hurt me rainy days, and I don't know what I want."

Mrs. Dallas smiled, as she replied, "You might make paper dolls, they are good rainy day people; that would be one thing. Then you can paint."

"I haven't but one brush, and I have used up all the books and papers you gave me to paint in."

"I can find some more, perhaps, and you and Florence can take turn about with the paint brush."

Dimple looked as if that would not suit very well, and

Florence seeing her look, felt a little hurt.

Paper dolls did not amuse them very long; and when Dimple was ready to color the pictures Mrs. Dallas had found for them, Florence declined absolutely to paint at all. So they both sat with their elbows on the window-sill, decidedly out of humor.

"Florence," said Dimple, presently, "I have an idea. Do you see that hogshead down there? It is running over."

"I see it," said Florence. "What of it; it isn't anything very wonderful."

"Well, you needn't be so disagreeable," said Dimple. "What I was going to say, is this; let's make paper boats, and put paper dolls in them. We can pretend the hogshead is Niagara Falls, and the water that runs down the gutter can be Niagara river."

"We will get sopping wet."

"Oh no, we won't; it isn't raining so awfully hard. I will put on my rubber waterproof, and you can put on mamma's. We can slip around there without any one seeing us, for mamma is busy on the other side of the house. Don't you think it would be fun?"

"Ye-es," said Florence, doubtfully.

"Let's hurry and make the boats then. Which paper dolls shall we take? The ugliest, I think, because they will all be drowned anyhow; and don't let's take any pretty frocks, because we can make dolls to fit the frocks when these are drowned."

With paper boats, dolls and waterproofs they stole softly down the front stairs, and shutting the door after them very gently, ran around the house to the hogshead. The roses were heavy with rain, and the honeysuckle shook big drops on them, as they ran by.

Amy E. Blanchard

The boats went topsy-turvy over the falls, upsetting the dolls, who went careering down the stream, to the great delight of the children.

They played till the last boat load was lost beyond all hope, and then, with wet feet and streaming sleeves, they crept back to the house.

"Now, what shall we do? It was lots of fun, Dimple," said Florence, "but I know your mother will scold, when she sees how wet our feet are, and your foot just well too, and see my sleeves. If we change our clothes she will wonder and then— What shall we do?"

"I don't think it was a bit of harm," said Dimple, determined to brave it out, "but it won't do to keep these wet frocks on. I know. We will go up into the attic, take them off, and hang them up to dry; then we can dress up in other things. There are trunks and boxes full of clothes up there, and we can play something."

"So we can," exclaimed Florence. "That is a perfectly lovely plan. Do you think our clothes will dry before supper?"

"Of course," said Dimple; "anyhow it will be funny to put on trains and things. Come on."

They raced up to the garret, and were soon diving into the boxes and trunks of winter clothing that Mrs. Dallas had packed away.

"Here," said Dimple, on her knees before a trunk, "take this skirt of mamma's," and she dragged out a cashmere skirt. "Florence, see what is in those band-boxes, and get us each a bonnet, while I hunt for a shawl or coat, or something."

After much tumbling up of clothing, she found what she wanted, and they had taken off their frocks when they heard Mrs. Dallas calling,

"Children, where are you?"

Both were silent for a moment, and stood with quickly beating hearts.

After a second call, Dimple mustered up courage to answer, "Up here, mamma."

"Where?"

"In the garret."

"What are you doing?"

"Just playing."

"Well, don't get into any mischief," came from the bottom of the stairs, and then Mrs. Dallas went off.

Presently there came another fright: a footstep on the stairs.

"Who is that?" asked Dimple, fearfully.

"Me," came the answer, as Bubbles' woolly head appeared.

"It is only Bubbles," said Dimple, much relieved. "Come up, Bubbles; we are dressing up, and you shall too; but if you dare to tell on us—off you go to the orphan asylum."

"I wouldn't tell fur nothin', Miss Dimple," said she, as Dimple threw her an old wrapper.

"I am going to be Lady Melrose, and Florence Lady Beckwith. You can be—Oh, Florence, let's dress Bubbles up in a coat and trousers, and have her for a footman."

"All right," said Florence, and shaking with laughter, Bubbles was attired in coat, trousers, and tall hat.

"Oh, she is too funny," said Florence, holding her sides. "Where is my bonnet?"

"That's mine," exclaimed Dimple, as Florence possessed herself of a bonnet with feathers in it.

"No, I chose this first," said Florence.

"Well, it's my mother's, I reckon, and I have the best right to it."

"Well, I'm company, and you're very impolite."

"I'm not," retorted Dimple, getting very red in the face.

"You are. I'd have my mother teach me how to behave, if I were you, Dimple Dallas."

"You horrid, red-headed thing!" cried Dimple, now thoroughly angry. "I'd like to know how you would look in a garnet velvet bonnet anyhow. You'd better take something that's not quite so near the color of your hair."

"My hair isn't red, it's auburn," said Florence, bursting into a sob, "and I'm not going to stay here another minute. I'm going straight home to my mother." And she tore off the clothes in which she had decked herself, leaving them in a heap on the floor. She snatched up her wet frock and ran downstairs.

Dimple sat quite still after Florence left her. She did not dare to go downstairs for fear of encountering her mother, and yet, suppose Florence should really mean to go home. How dreadful! She considered the question till she could bear it no longer, and, slowly putting on her own clothes, she crept downstairs, hoping as she went from room to room that she would find Florence. She even peeped cautiously in upon her mother, busy with her sewing, but no Florence was to be seen.

"Perhaps she has started to go home," Dimple said to herself, in real alarm. "Oh, dear, I hope there hasn't been any train along that she could take." She put on her hat, seized an umbrella from the rack, and sallied forth. It was still raining hard, and as she splashed along, the little girl was very miserable.

It was quite a walk to the railway station, and Dimple hurried her steps, fearing she might be too late to intercept her cousin. She entered the waiting-room of the station, and looked anxiously around. No Florence was there. Her heart sank and she turned to go. Florence had really meant what she said. And her aunt and cousins in Baltimore, what would they think of her? The tears began to roll down Dimple's cheeks as she looked up and down the long track. She did not know what to do next. It would be so dreadful to go home and tell her mother that she had driven her cousin away by her rudeness. She was about to turn toward home, when she bethought herself of making some inquiry about the trains; and she entered the waiting-room again.

Standing on tiptoe she asked the ticket agent. "When was the last train to Baltimore?"

"Next train leaves at 4:50," said the man, without looking up.

"Not the next train, but the last train. When did it go?"

"Last train!" the man glanced up. "Last train left at 2:15."

"Thank you." It was with a sense of relief that she heard him give the time. Florence had not left the house so long ago as that. It was now after four, and two hours had not elapsed since they were playing in the garret. So she went slowly out, but suddenly remembered that Florence was not at home. Where was she? Perhaps she was lost. She didn't know her way about very well, Dimple reflected, and she could easily have taken a wrong turn.

"I'll just have to look for her, that's all," thought Dimple; and the little feet pattered along in the rain, getting wetter and wetter each moment.

Up one street and down another went Dimple, but there was no sign of Florence, and the child's repentance grew stronger as she traveled on. Her imagination saw Florence in a dozen different plights, each one worse than the last. Accidents of various kinds, disasters of every possible nature, even the very improbable idea that she had been stolen by gypsies, rose to the child's mind, till, terror stricken, she flew along, scarcely knowing which way she went.

She was conscious of steadily pursuing footsteps behind her, but she did not turn to look until the feet came nearer and nearer and a soft plaintive voice called, "Oh, Miss Dimple, stop, please stop." Looking around, she saw that Bubbles had followed her.

It was a relief to see the familiar face, and Dimple forlornly dropped into her little maid's arms crying: "Oh, Bubbles! Oh, Bubbles, Florence is lost."

"No 'm, she ain't," replied Bubbles, with confidence.

"Oh, how do you know?"

"Cause she come in de front do' jis' as I was gwine th'ough de yard. I never stopped to ast her nothin', fo' I seen yuh a kitin' down street, an' I put after yuh, lickety-split. All of a suddent I los' sight of yuh, an' I been a standin' on de cornah waitin' fo' yuh to come back. I know yuh 'bleedged to cross to git home, an' I been a waitin' fo' yuh."

"Oh Bubbles! Oh Bubbles! I'm so glad, but I'm so tired and so wet, and—oh dear—I'm afraid to tell mamma, and I'm so miserable. I never was so miserable."

Bubbles looked as sympathetic as the occasion required, and trotted along by Dimple's side, holding the umbrella over her, and trying to suggest all manner of comforting things.

"Hit'll all be ovah befo' yuh is twict married, Miss Dimple, and hit mought be wuss. S'posin' Miss Flo'ence was los' sho 'nough, den yuh might tek on. She safe an' soun'. Jes' yuh come in de back way, an' I'll git yuh some dry things. An' Sylvy won't say nothin'. I jes' know she wont, an' yuh can git dry by de kitchen fire. I reckon Miss Flo'ence mighty 'shamed o' herse'f, kickin' up all dis rumpus 'bout nothin'."

But Dimple shook her head. "It wasn't about nothing. I behaved just as mean as could be, and I'm the one to be ashamed. I'll go straight to mamma; it will be best, for she would find out anyhow, and besides, I'd feel a great deal worse if I deceived her about it."

Bubbles was not to be convinced that her beloved Miss Dimple was at all in the wrong, but Dimple would not change her mind, being in a state of great humility and penitence, and finally Bubbles gave up trying to dissuade her.

Florence had reached home long before. Indeed she had not gone very far before her anger cooled, although she was still very much hurt; but she concluded it would not be right to start off for her own home without a word to her aunt, who had been so kind to her. This thought added to her unhappiness, and she went to Dimple's room, throwing herself on the floor, crying bitterly.

The sound of her sobs brought Mrs. Dallas from the next room.

"Why, Florence," she said, seeing the little girl prone upon the floor. "What is the matter? Why have you taken off your frock?"

"Oh! auntie," sobbed Florence, "please let me go home; indeed, I can't stay."

"Are you homesick?" asked her aunt, as she took her up on her lap, and pushed back the damp hair from her face. "Poor little girl!"

A fresh burst of tears was the only answer.

"Where is Dimple?" asked Mrs. Dallas.

But Florence only cried the harder, and her aunt was forced to put her down with an uncomfortable sense of there being something wrong. She went directly up to the attic, but it was silent. Dimple was not there, neither was Bubbles, and no amount of search revealed them. She went back to Florence, who dried her tears and unburdened her heart, and then in her turn became alarmed about Dimple, since no amount of hunting disclosed her whereabouts.

Mrs. Dallas was, herself, becoming much worried, when the door slowly opened and a disheveled little figure stood before them, with soaking garments and sodden shoes.

For a moment Dimple stood, then ran forward and buried her head in her mother's lap.

"Mamma," she sobbed, "it was all on account of the weather. I coaxed Florence out to the hogshead, and then we got wet, and didn't know how to get out of it, and we went up into the attic, and I felt naughty all the time, and we got mad, and oh dear! I wish the sun would shine."

"I am afraid from all I hear, that you have been the one to set all this mischief astir," said her mother. "I thought I could trust my little girl. Think, Dimple, what a day's work. You have tempted your cousin to do wrong, first by going out in the wet, and again by meddling with the clothing upstairs; then you hurt her feelings, and quarreled with her, and now you blame the weather for it all, besides setting a bad example to Bubbles. Where have you been, my child?"

"Trying to find Florence, mamma. I walked and walked, and I was so worried, and—oh, mamma, I thought all sorts of dreadful things. I went to the station, Florence, and I found out there that you hadn't really gone home; then I thought you were lost, or that the cars had run over you, or the gypsies had stolen you, or that—oh I'm so miserable," she caught her breath, and shivered with cold and excitement.

Her mother was unfastening her wet garments. She felt that Dimple's naughtiness had brought its own punishment. "I think Florence has changed her mind about going home," she said, quietly.

Dimple raised a tear-stained face. "Oh, Florence, have you?" she exclaimed. "I'm so glad. I don't want you to think I don't love you, for I do. I love you dearly, dearly, Florence, and I think your hair is lovely."

This was too much for Florence's tender heart, and she sobbed out, "It was my fault too, Dimple. I said hateful things, and I couldn't forgive myself when I thought you had gone, I didn't know where. I had no business to scare you so. Please, Aunt Flo, kiss us and forgive us, and please, for my sake, don't scold Dimple."

Mrs. Dallas gathered the two little penitents into her loving arms. They were so truly sorry, and had suffered really more than they deserved. "I think Dimple sees her fault quite plainly, dear," Florence was told, "but I am afraid you will both be ill, and so I think I must put you to bed, not for punishment, but because you must be kept warm, and must have something hot to keep you from taking cold. Where is Bubbles, Dimple? Wasn't she with you?"

"Not all the time, mamma, but she came after me, and found me on the corner. Please don't punish her. She only went out because she wanted to find me."

"I understand that, and I know she did not mean to do wrong.

Amy E. Blanchard

She did what she felt to be her duty to you. I'll not scold her, nor punish her, daughter."

Dimple gave a sigh of relief, and pressed her wet cheek against her mother's. "Please kiss me, mamma," she whispered, "and then I'll know you forgive naughty me."

Mrs. Dallas immediately consented, and when she left the room, two very contrite little girls cuddled up close to each other, and took without a murmur the hot herb tea which Mrs. Dallas brought to them. And the next morning when they woke, lo! the sun was shining, and not an ache nor a pain did either little girl feel to remind her of the dreary yesterday.

CHAPTER IV

HOUSEBREAKERS

Despite all this unpleasant experience, it was only about a week later that Dimple and Florence came near getting into trouble again. This time, however, it was Florence who set the ball rolling. It was not exactly from a spirit of mischief, but because her fancy was appealed to, and because she did not see any harm in what she proposed.

The two little girls had been to take a note to Mrs. Hardy, and on their way home they passed a pretty house and grounds which greatly attracted Florence.

"Oh, do let us stop and look in," she said. "I think this is the very prettiest place here, don't you, Dimple?"

"Yes," was the reply, "I like it best. The grounds are so lovely. See those roses."

The two pressed their faces against the iron railing, and let their eyes wander over the lawn and to the garden beyond.

"How very quiet it is," Florence remarked, presently. "We can't hear a sound except the wind among the trees, and the robins singing. There doesn't seem to be a soul about. Who lives here, Dimple?"

"The Atkinsons. Mamma and papa know them."

Amy E. Blanchard

"Are there any little children?"

"Not now; there used to be a little girl named Stella, but she died two years ago, and now there is only their eldest son living; he has just gone abroad with his mother. That is why it's so quiet. They are all away. You see the house is shut up."

"Ah, I wonder if they would mind if we went in and looked around. Do you think they would mind? I should love so to go and sit on that porch for a few minutes."

Dimple hesitated. She wasn't quite sure that it would be right for them to go in, especially when no one was at home.

"You know," Florence went on, "it would be just exactly the same as if we went there to call, and they should happen to be out. It won't hurt anybody or anything for us to walk around and look at the grounds."

At last Dimple consented. So they lifted the latch of the gate and shut it behind them very gingerly.

"Do you often come here?" asked Florence, when they had made their tour of the grounds and were sitting on the porch in the shadow of the vines.

"Not so very often, but I have been here with mamma when she came to call. I remember Stella very well. She died of diphtheria, and they have a lovely portrait of her. She was such a pretty little girl, and the portrait shows her with a great big dog she used to have."

"How I should like to see the portrait. Wouldn't it be nice if the door should suddenly open, and we could walk right in?"

Dimple laughed. "I'd be scared if that should happen. The house is beautiful inside. I never saw so many pretty things. Mrs. Atkinson's father was a naval officer, and she has curiosities from all over the world."

"I wish Mrs. Atkinson had said, 'Dimple, here are the keys, come in as often as you like while we are away; in fact, I wish you would try to come in and look around once in a while to see if everything is all right.'"

"Maybe she would have said that if she had thought of it," returned Dimple, "for she is always so nice and pleasant."

Florence cast wistful eyes up and down the side of the house; then she went out on the lawn, at the side, and looked up. "Dimple, come here," she called, and her cousin obeyed. "We could get in as easily as anything," said Florence. "See, that's a very easy tree to climb, and that long branch goes right over the upper porch. We could reach that; then we could go in by raising the window."

"If the window is not fastened down. Maybe there is some one in the house, after all. I shouldn't think they would leave it with no one ever to look after it. We might go around to the back door and see."

"Let's try climbing the tree anyhow. It will be easy enough to do that, and won't do a bit of harm. See, I'm going," and Florence put her foot against the rough bark, and swung herself up, reaching the porch without difficulty. But Dimple would not follow and her cousin climbed down again, not, however, as easily as she had gone up.

"It was nothing at all to do," she declared. "I think you might try it, Dimple. I'll tell you what we'll do: let's bring our dolls to-morrow, and go up there and play. I'm sure if I had a pretty place like this, I should be glad if two little girls, like us, could come and enjoy it. Ah, Dimple, you don't know how fine it is on that upper porch. It would be the finest place in the world to play in."

The idea took such possession of her that the next morning she broached the subject again.

"I'll ask mamma," said Dimple, at last consenting with this proviso. But Mrs. Dallas had gone out to spend the morning with a friend, and finally Florence's persuasions overcame Dimple's scruples, and with Celestine and Rubina they set forth.

At first Florence was contented to play on the corner porch, but the memory of the day before was too much for her, and she again climbed to the upper porch. "Do come up, Dimple," she coaxed. "You've no idea how fine it is, with the tree all around. It's just like a nest," and Dimple decided that she would try it too.

"Wait, we mustn't leave the dolls," Florence said. "I wish we had a piece of string. See if you can find a piece, Dimple."

After much searching Dimple hunted up an end of rope, which she found by the kitchen shed, and brought around. "Will this do?" she asked.

"Finely. Can you throw it so I can catch it?"

"I don't know. Maybe I could if I tied a stone to it. Don't let it hit you, Florence."

After several attempts the rope was landed, and when the dolls were fastened to it, they were drawn safely up, and then Dimple made her ascent successfully.

"It is nice," she declared. "Isn't it fun to be here, where no one can see us? I wonder if that window will open." She gave the shutters a little shake and lo! they offered no resistance, but opened easily, and, the latch being out of order, the window, too, yielded to their efforts, and before they knew it, they were inside.

"Now we're here, we might as well go through the house," said Florence. "And you can show me the portrait."

They proceeded stealthily through rooms whose furniture was swathed in sheets to keep away the dust. It all looked rather bare and desolate upstairs in the dim rooms, but it was better below, especially in the dining-room, where a big bay window let in a flood of light when the inside shutters were opened.

"Let's pretend it's our house, and keep house really," Florence exclaimed. "Here is a broom and a duster. I'll sweep and you can dust. Then if we can find some dishes, we'll set the table. I wish we had brought something to eat. Oh, Dimple, you haven't shown me the portrait yet; where is it?"

"In the library. Come, we'll go there now."

"My, but it's dark in here!" Florence exclaimed, as they entered the room. "Let us open the shutters a little so we can see the picture."

This they managed to do, shutting the window carefully.

"It seems dark still," Dimple remarked. "I wonder what makes this such a dark room." Just then they heard a mighty crash and both started, then clung to each other, whispering, "What's that?"

"It is thunder," said Dimple, when a second peal was heard. "Oh, how dark it is. Come, Florence; we must hurry. Open the window and shut the shutters as quick as you can and I'll go to the dining-room. We must leave everything as we found it."

"Don't leave me," Florence implored. "I can't bear to be alone when the lightning flashes so." And together they fastened the shutters and the windows, then ran to the porch, where they had left their dolls.

An angry gust was blowing the dust about furiously. The trees swayed and creaked, lashing their branches about in a very terrifying way. The thunder growled and muttered, while sharp flashes of lightning zigzagged across the sky almost incessantly.

"We would never dare to go down the tree while it is blowing so," said Florence, after they had surveyed the scene for a moment in silence.

"But it is beginning to rain. Oh, dear! What shall we do? It's coming down a perfect torrent. Come back, Florence; we'll have to go inside," cried Dimple. And snatching up their dolls, they retreated into the house in no enviable state of mind, between fear of the tempest and alarm at being obliged to stay alone where they were.

"We might as well make ourselves comfortable," Florence said at last. "Suppose we go down to the library or the dining-room. We can open the inside shutters, and it won't seem so gloomy. I'd rather see the lightning than stay up here in the dark."

"Oh, dear! I wish we hadn't come at all," sighed Dimple. "I wish we were safe at home. Mamma will be so worried, for she won't know where we are. I do wish we hadn't come."

Florence was very uncomfortable, but she tried to brave it out. "Anyhow," she said, "it's a great deal better than to be out in the storm. I am sure auntie will be very glad when she knows we were safe here, and it isn't as if you had come to a perfectly strange house. The Atkinsons are your friends, and they won't mind a bit our coming here for shelter. I know they won't. They'd be very hard-hearted if they did mind."

"Yes, I s'pose so," returned Dimple, somewhat comforted.

"Very likely your mamma isn't bothering at all about us," Florence went on. "She probably hasn't gone home herself, on account of the storm."

They had been conversing together at the top of the stairs, and now made their way to the dining-room, where, after opening the shutters, they stood looking out at the rain. The peals of thunder had died away into distant mutterings, but it was still raining hard.

"Somehow we always get into trouble when it rains," Dimple remarked.

"Don't let's talk about that," returned Florence. "See how the raindrops dance up and down. Little water fairies they are. Don't they look as if they were having a good time?"

"Yes; but I'm getting hungry. I wonder if it isn't most dinner time. Do you suppose it will rain all afternoon, Florence?"

"I don't know. If it holds up we'll have to run between the drops."

"But how can we get out? We could never climb down that sopping wet tree, and we would be very wicked to leave any part of the house down here unfastened. Some one might see us and try to get in."

They lapsed into a grave silence which was presently broken by a startled "What's that?" from Dimple. She heard a sound like the click of a key turning in a latch. They listened fearfully, as the sound was followed by the shutting of a door, and the noise of footsteps along the hall. The two girls looked at each other. "Let's hide," whispered Florence, but before they had decided what to do, a man was seen standing in the doorway. It was Mr. Atkinson.

"Well, well, well," he exclaimed, "where did you little girls come from? You came in out of the rain, I suppose, but how did you manage it? Why, Eleanor, is it you? I declare, I didn't know you. It is fortunate you managed to escape the storm; it was a hard one."

Dimple stood very much confused, her color coming and

going, and her eyes very bright. But she summoned up courage to make the confession: "We did come in out of the rain, Mr. Atkinson, but no one let us in, and we didn't happen to come here on account of the storm."

"You didn't! Come here, then, and tell me about it." He drew her to his side and looked down at her very kindly.

She dropped her eyes and hung her head in confusion, but she went on, "We,—we thought it was so pretty here, and—and we thought you wouldn't mind if we came and brought our dolls and sat on the porch a little while; we didn't think you'd care if we were very good and didn't touch anything. Then it was so easy to climb the tree and get on the other porch, and when we got there,—why I wanted to show Florence the portrait of your little girl, and we did not have to force the shutter at all; it opened just as easy, and so did the window; and we went downstairs, and while we were looking at the portrait the storm came up and we were afraid to climb down the tree; it was blowing about so, and we didn't like to go out any other way and leave the windows downstairs unfastened. So—we stayed."

Mr. Atkinson listened quietly. "So you were housebreakers. Don't you know that's a prison offence? Burglary is a pretty serious crime." He looked very serious, and Dimple did not see the twinkle in his eyes. Her own grew round with horror.

"Oh!" she gasped. "Oh! we didn't mean—" The tears began to gather, and the child's lips quivered. She was overcome with dismay. "I am so sorry, so dreadfully sorry," she quavered.

Mr. Atkinson put his hand on her sunny head. "There, dear, never mind," he said, "you were a very innocent pair of housebreakers, and you are a very brave and honest little girl to tell me the truth about it, when you might easily have allowed me to think it happened another way. Of course, on general principles, it isn't right to break into any one's house, but I think you may have done me a good turn by letting me know about that weak place upstairs, and you may have prevented a real thief from breaking in. You see, I come down from the city every Saturday to look after things while my wife and son are away, and I am glad I happened to be here just now. Let us forget all about the unpleasant part of this, and make ourselves comfortable. You are my guests. Who is your little friend?"

"My cousin Florence."

"Ah, yes. I am glad to see you, Florence. Now don't you think it would be wise, Eleanor, if I were to speak to your father over the 'phone, and let him know you are safe?"

"Oh, yes, thank you. Is there a telephone in the house?"

"Yes, and I can call up your father at his office. You can speak to him yourself, if you like. What time does he go home to dinner?"

"About half-past one o'clock."

Mr. Atkinson consulted his watch. "We shall catch him, I think." And in a few minutes Dimple, listening, heard her father's voice in reply to Mr. Atkinson's "Hallo! is that you, Dallas?"

"Don't you want to speak to him yourself?" asked Mr. Atkinson, when he had told Mr. Dallas that Dimple and her cousin were safely housed. He lifted the little girl up so she could call her father. "I'm safe here, papa, and so is Florence," she said; "please tell mamma."

The answer came, "I will, daughter; I'm glad you are in good hands. I'll tell mamma to send Bubbles for you when it has stopped raining."

"Let them stay till I take them home," spoke up Mr. Atkinson. "I can take care of them, and it will be a great pleasure to have them here."

Amy E. Blanchard

"Very well, if you like. I shall be satisfied to have them in such safe hands. Good-bye," came Mr. Dallas's parting words.

"Good-bye," and Mr. Atkinson hung up the receiver, and turned to his guests. "Now, young ladies, I suspect you are hungry. I am, for one. Suppose we see what we can find to eat." He took out his keys and unlocked the pantry door. The girls looked at each other. There were delightful possibilities before them.

"I'll forage in here," continued Mr. Atkinson, "while you set the table. You'll find dishes in there." And he pointed to a china-closet.

This was such an unexpected outcome of the morning's affair, that the two little girls retired behind the door and hugged each other, and then briskly went to work to set the table, upon which Mr. Atkinson placed various articles.

"I keep a lot of such truck in here," he told them. "So, in case I get hungry, I can find a bite to eat. Do you like sardines or canned salmon best?"

"Sardines!" exclaimed both the girls.

"That settles it. We haven't any ice, or we could have some lemonade. We'd better have chocolate. What do you say?"

"It would be very nice, but we have no fire."

"Fire enough. See here." He turned on the gas, and lighted a little stove over which the chocolate was made, condensed milk being at hand for use.

"Now, let me see. I've some ginger-snaps somewhere, and some marmalade. This is rather a mixed meal, I am thinking, but it will keep us from starving."

"I should think so," said Florence, surveying the table. "I think it is fine."

"And we can wash the dishes afterward. Will you let us?" asked Dimple.

"I shall be charmed to have you," Mr. Atkinson assured her. "It was one of the points upon which I felt uncertain. I confess to disliking, very much, that part of the business; and now you relieve my anxiety."

They made a merry meal of it, and became very well acquainted with their host before it was over. He told them funny stories and kept them laughing so that they were a long time getting their appetites satisfied, and as it had become much cooler, Bubbles appeared with wraps for them before they had finished with the dishes.

"We have had such a lovely, lovely time," said Dimple, as she raised a beaming face to Mr. Atkinson. "You know just what to do to make little girls have a good time, don't you?"

He stooped and kissed her. "I had a little girl once," he replied, gravely.

Dimple put her two arms closely around his neck. She felt so very, very sorry when she remembered pretty little Stella. "I'd like to be your little girl, if I had to be any one's but papa's and mamma's," she whispered.

"Thank you, dear child, I appreciate that. It is a very great compliment," he answered, slowly. "I want you two little girls to come over whenever you can. I am always here on Saturday afternoons. Will you come to see me often?"

"If mamma will let us. I'm afraid maybe she will not, because we were naughty about coming when we had no right to."

"Well, we'll see how we can manage it. I will tell your father about it, myself, or, better still, I will walk home with you, and you can tell your story to your mother, and let me beg pardon for you. How will that do?"

Dimple's eyes spoke her thanks, and she turned to Florence who answered with a satisfied smile.

And so by Mr. Atkinson's kind request the culprits were forgiven, and were promised that they should go again since Mr. Atkinson really wanted them. "And you must feel at liberty to play about the grounds all you choose," he told the girls. "They can run about, and sit on the porches and do as they please, so long as they do not trample the flower-beds, or get into any mischief," he said to Mrs. Dallas.

"We wouldn't hurt anything for the world," put in Florence and Dimple, eagerly. And they bade their good friend farewell, feeling very humble and thankful that matters had turned out so well for them.

"We don't deserve it, and I feel dreadfully ashamed of myself," said Florence, meekly.

"I think Mr. Atkinson put our heads in the fire," said Dimple, soberly.

"What do you mean?" her mother asked.

"Why, isn't that what the Bible says when any one does something very kind to you after you have been mean to him?"

Mrs. Dallas laughed. "You mean he heaped coals of fire on your head; that is the expression the Bible uses."

"It's a funny one," Dimple responded, thoughtfully. "Anyhow, mamma, I shall never, never try to break into any one's house again."

"I hope not."

"I really meant to ask you if we could go over there, mamma, but you had gone out. We were in a dreadful trouble for a while."

"Yes, I know, dear. One very little wrong beginning sometimes leads to a great deal of trouble; even grown people find that out."

"Do they? It always seems as if you must know everything, mamma."

She smiled and shook her head. Thus ended this incident, but neither Dimple nor Florence ever forgot it.

CHAPTER V

ROCK

Florence and Dimple with Rubina and Celestine were on the back porch, when they heard some one whistle, and looking up they saw Rock coming around the corner of the house.

"Good-morning," said he, "I am glad you have your dolls here; I want to measure them."

"Why, are you a tailor?" asked Florence.

"No," he said, laughing, "only a cabinetmaker. I came over with a message from my mother to Mrs. Dallas, and a message from myself to yourselves."

"Have you given mamma her message?" asked Dimple.

"Yes," said he, "and mine is that I want you to come to tea with me to-morrow evening, you and Florence and the dolls."

"Oh, the dolls?"

"Yes, the dolls. I will come for you, if you like, at half-past four."

"Did mamma say we might go?"

"Yes, so it is all settled."

"Now," said Florence, "we *must* make the dolls new frocks. Do tell us, Rock, what they ought to wear."

Rock turned over the bits of stuff in Dimple's box. "White, I think," said he; "that dotted stuff is pretty."

"Oh, yes," said Dimple, "and I have plenty of that. We can trim them with this lace, Florence, and they will look so cool and nice. Now if mamma only had time to make hats for them!"

"I'll make them hats," said Rock.

"You! Whoever heard of boys making hats for dolls?"

"Did you never hear of a man-milliner?" asked Rock. "And men dressmakers? I have. You stay here. I am going to ask your mamma for something to make them of."

"Isn't he a funny boy, Florence?" said Dimple, as Rock disappeared; "but I think he is real nice. Just hand me the scissors, won't you? Which way does this go, so, or so?"

"So, like mine. Are you going to make a wide or a narrow hem?"

"Wide, if the stuff is long enough; it isn't so easy, but it looks nicer. I wonder if mamma will give us fresh ribbons for sashes for the dolls; it will set them off so."

"Here comes Rock," exclaimed Florence, "and what has he in his hand? An old bonnet, I declare."

"Now," said Rock, "if you will tell me where I can get a basin of water, I will make the hats."

"With water?"

"I shall need water. Don't get up—Bubbles will get it for me,"

Amy E. Blanchard

as Dimple was about to put down her work.

Bubbles brought the water, and Rock began to rip the straw bonnet to pieces; then he dampened it a little and sewed it into shape, once in a while dampening it more to give it the right turn. "Will you have a wide or a narrow brim?" he asked.

"Oh, just a between brim. Don't you say so, Florence? Isn't it going to be lovely? Did you ever?" as Rock handed her a cunning little straw hat.

"Now for the other one," said he, and he soon had that done too.

A little narrow ribbon and one or two flowers made the hats perfect.

"Oh, Rock, I wish you were my brother," sighed Dimple, as she held her doll off at arm's length to admire her. "Rubina, you are a darling! Blue is *so* becoming to her."

"I almost wish I had trimmed mine with blue," said Florence, regretfully.

"Oh, I think pink is just as pretty," exclaimed Rock, "and it is nicer not to have them both alike."

"Now what are you making?" asked Dimple, as Rock went on sewing straw.

"Baskets."

"Baskets, for the dolls?"

"Yes, for the dolls, or you either."

Dimple put her chin in her hands, and leaned on the arm of her chair to watch him.

"How clever you are," she said, "I wish you were my brother, really and truly, Rock."

"Well, we will pretend I am," said he. "What shall I put in your basket, sister?"

They all laughed.

"I don't think it will hold much, but Rubina can put her work in it. See, if I pin her arm up so, she can hold it nicely. There! I must go and show it to mamma. I'll tell her to adopt you," she called back, as she ran off.

"Now I must clear up my scraps," said Rock, as he put the finishing touches to the other basket.

"Mamma says I may gather you some flowers," said Dimple, coming out again with a pair of shears in her hand, "and she says you are a very nice boy, a very nice boy indeed."

Rock laughed. "She wouldn't think so sometimes," said he. "I don't believe she wants to change children with my mother."

"I hope she doesn't want to," said Dimple, then added quickly, "Not that I don't think your mother is real nice, Rock, but you know I am so used to mine, and she is so used to me."

"Of course," said Rock, laughing again. "I didn't mean they would change, or even think of it."

"Now let's get the flowers," said Dimple; "you are to choose just which you like best, Rock," she said, leading the way to the flower-beds. "The pansies are almost gone, but there are plenty of roses yet, and verbenas, and mignonette, and lots of things."

"Now, Rock," she said, as they went along the paths, "you are not choosing the prettiest ones at all. I believe you are picking out the mean ones on purpose; I am going to choose myself.

You tell me, Florence, whenever you see a real pretty one."

Florence promised, and Rock looked on, secretly pleased that they had taken the matter into their own hands.

"What lovely ones you have chosen," he said, as Dimple gave the bunch into his hands. "Thank you so much."

"And thank you, so much," said the girls, "for the hats, and the baskets, and the invitation."

"You will be sure to be ready," he said, at the gate.

"Yes," they cried.

"At half-past four?"

"Yes."

"Good-bye sister; good-bye Florence; go in out of the sun."

"Good-bye, brother, keep in the shade."

Then they laughed and ran in.

"Mamma," cried Dimple. "Auntie," cried Florence, "where are you?"

"Upstairs," she answered.

Up they ran. "Aren't you glad Rock is such a nice boy? Did you know boys could be so nice?" asked Dimple.

"I knew they could be, if they would."

"What makes Rock so gentle and kind and good?"

"Well, you see he lost his father when he was a very little boy, and as he had no brothers or sisters, he has been almost constantly with his mother, who is a very gentle, sweet woman."

"He doesn't seem silly, like some boys, either," said Florence. "I know a boy, we call him 'sissy,' he is so like a girl, and he is always whining, and afraid of cold, and afraid of sun, and afraid of everything."

"I shouldn't like that kind of boy," Dimple said. "Mamma, I call Rock my brother, and he calls me sister."

"Do you?" said her mother, smiling. "Now it is nearly dinner time, and if I am not mistaken, two little girls have left their new dolls, and all their scraps and things out on the porch."

"So we have!" they exclaimed, and ran down to bring them in.

The dolls were laid away in state for the next day, and at the sound of the dinner bell, the girls went into dinner.

Since the arrival of Florence, Dimple had not cared so much for Bubbles' society, and sometimes objected to her joining in their plays; but Bubbles, by the gift of Floridy Alabamy, did not lack amusement, and could be seen almost any afternoon happy with her doll.

She was singing, "Oh Beurah lan', sweet Beurah lan'," when Florence called her.

"What are you singing, Bubbles?"

"Beurah lan'," answered she.

"What does she mean, Dimple?"

"Beulah land. She does get things so twisted. We are going down to the woodshed to play till mamma calls us. Bubbles, do you want to go?"

Of course Bubbles did, and off they all went.

The woodshed was at some distance from the house, out in a shady place. Sometimes the children took to the roof, which could be reached by a ladder, and it was the scene of many a bold adventure.

"What shall we play?" said one to another.

"Injun," suggested Bubbles.

"No Indian for me, since my foot was cut," said Dimple.

"Let's play house afire and climb from the roof by the ladder," said Florence.

"No. I tell you," said Dimple, "let's be cats and get on the roof and meow like they do at night."

They all laughed at this, but finally concluded to be birds, and build nests, but why they should take leaves in their mouths and climb up and down the ladder no mortal could tell, and indeed this proved too tedious a play, and they all sat on the roof to decide what should be done next.

Suddenly Dimple cried out, "What is that sticking out of your pocket, Bubbles?"

Bubbles quickly thrust whatever it was back into her pocket, and was about to get down from the roof, when Dimple held her.

"Pull it out, Florence," she cried. "I believe it is a piece of my dotted swiss."

And so it was. Bubbles had been consumed with envy ever since Rubina and Celestine had been dressed in white, and wanted her doll to look as well.

"You wicked girl! where did you get it?" asked Dimple, fiercely.

"Found it."

"You didn't. You've been stealing. You stole it from my box that I left on the porch yesterday. What were you going to do with it?"

"Make a frock for Floridy Alabamy."

"Why didn't you ask for something, instead of taking what didn't belong to you?"

Bubbles was silent.

"You told a story too, when you said you found it; you knew it was mine. Now you shall be punished."

"Don't send me to the orphan asylum," said Bubbles, beginning to cry.

"No, I promised mamma I wouldn't say that any more, but I shall do something. The idea of your doing such a thing. I really used to think you were nearly as nice as a white girl, Bubbles, but I never shall any more."

Bubbles cried harder than ever at this.

"What shall I do with her, Florence?"

"Take her doll away," suggested she.

"No! no! no! please, Miss Dimple, I'll never do so no mo'," cried Bubbles, "'deed an' 'deed, I won't. Don't take my doll away. Yuh can whup me, or anything, but don't tek my doll away," and she hugged it tightly, rocking herself to and fro.

Dimple thought a moment, and then she said, "I know, we

will leave her here on the roof, and take the ladder away; then when mamma calls us to come in to dress we can put the ladder up again, and she can get down."

This was agreed upon, and Bubbles was left a lofty prisoner.

The girls concluded to play under the big tree, and became so interested, that when Mrs. Dallas called them, they forgot all about Bubbles, and went into the house without ever putting up the ladder.

"What am I to wear, mamma?" asked Dimple. "One of my white frocks, I suppose."

"Yes," said her mother.

"And Florence too? Yes, Florence, then we will all be in white, the dolls too. Mamma, may we carry our parasols?"

"I don't think you will need them. Now, girls, I will send papa for you at half-past eight. I hope you will be little ladies, both of you, because I particularly want Mrs. Hardy to be fond of you."

"Oh, we will, mamma," replied Dimple. "Why do you want Mrs. Hardy to like us?"

"I have two or three reasons. I will tell you when we have more time. Hurry, Florence, and put on your frock; it is nearly half-past four."

"I hear a carriage stopping," said Dimple, running to look out of the window. "Florence, Florence, do hurry; Rock and his mother are out there in a carriage; where are the dolls? Oh, here they are. No, I have yours," she exclaimed, excitedly. "Do, Florence, get your hat."

"Don't get so excited, Dimple," said her mamma. "There is no need of such a very great hurry as all that. I will go down and you can come. You have forgotten your handkerchief; it is there on the bureau."

"Oh Dimple, do get me a handkerchief too," said Florence, "I don't know what does make me so behindhand."

"Perfume, Florence?"

"Oh, please, just a wee drop, not too much."

"Cologne or violet water?"

"Which have you?"

"Cologne."

"Then I will take the other. Now I'm ready. Do you suppose we are going anywhere? It is such a little way to drive only to the house."

"I don't know," returned Dimple. "We'll soon see."

"We thought it was so early," said Mrs. Hardy, "that we could take a short drive before tea, if these little girls would like it."

"Indeed we should," said they.

"Then help them in, Rock," and they were soon seated, driving off in great style, dolls and all.

Meanwhile, Bubbles sat on the roof, waiting for their return. As the time passed and they did not come, she made desperate efforts to get down, but there was no way. The tree that shaded the woodhouse was just too high to reach, and she crept to the edge of the roof, making up her mind to jump, but when she saw the distance her heart failed her, and she went back.

"Leave me hyah all night I s'pose," she said, "mebbe I'll ketch cold and die; 'most wisht I would."

Amy E. Blanchard

Then she heard some one call "Bubbles, Bubbles," but though she answered, no one came.

It grew later and later, the sun went down, and the sky sent up little puffs of pink clouds overhead.

Bubbles lay down on her back, and looked up at the sky. After a while a little star peeped out, then disappeared again, like a baby playing "Peep-bo."

"Angels, I reckon," thought Bubbles. "S'pose I won't git to see 'em. I reckon stealin's awful," and she lay there in a very humble frame of mind, till she went to sleep.

"I cannot imagine what has become of Bubbles," said Mrs. Dallas to her husband when he came in. "I have looked the house over, and called her in every room. She cannot have followed the children. I never knew her to stay away before."

"Hasn't Sylvy seen her?"

"Not since early in the afternoon. She has looked all over the place." And so she had, but Bubbles asleep on the roof did not hear her, and a limb of the tree on that side hid her from view.

"There is no reason for her running off, is there?" asked Mr. Dallas.

"No, unless Dimple has threatened her with the orphan asylum once too often. She has such a horror of it, but I told Dimple not to do so again, and she is not apt to disobey."

They sat down to tea, and it was not till an hour later that Bubbles was rescued. Mr. Dallas was walking about, smoking his cigar, when he heard a doleful voice saying,

"Lordy, Lordy, I'm awful bad, just as well go to the orphan asylum. I'll die hyah, plum sho'."

He listened, and walked a few steps further.

"Wisht I was a bird, I'd get up in that tree. Wisht I had a raven to bring me my supper—s'pose I'll starve and die too."

"Bubbles, where are you?" called Mr. Dallas. He heard a scrambling overhead, and a delighted reply.

"Hyah, sah, hyah I are."

He looked all around, but did not see her.

"Where are you?" he asked again.

"On de roof, sah."

"Well, why don't you get down?"

"Ain't no way, sah; done tucken de ladder away."

Mr. Dallas found the ladder and put it up, and Bubbles scrambled down.

"Have you been up there all this time?"

"Yas, sah," said Bubbles, scraping one foot with the bare toes of the other.

"How came the ladder down?"

"Miss Dimple done did it."

"What for?"

Bubbles hung her head, and began scraping the other foot.

"What for?" again asked Mr. Dallas.

"I done stole," said Bubbles, solemnly.

"And she did it to punish you?"

"Yas, sah."

Mr. Dallas could not avoid smiling, but he said, "Go along into the house, and tell Mrs. Dallas about it. By the way, didn't you see any one looking for you?"

"No, sah. I was clean tuckered a waitin', and I went to sleep. 'Specs they came then mebbe."

"Well, go along," he said, and Bubbles started for the house, while he went to bring home the girls.

CHAPTER VI

THE TEA-PARTY

When the carriage left the house Mrs. Hardy directed the driver to go through one of the pleasant roads leading from the town.

"Which is your favorite drive, Dimple?" she asked.

"Oh, Pleasant Valley and Big Run," answered she. "Don't you think so?"

"I hardly know," said Mrs. Hardy. "I have been around so little; you will have to be our guide and tell us the pretty places."

Dimple felt quite important, and chatted away at a great rate.

"Didn't Rock make our dolls pretty hats?" she asked. "Mrs. Hardy, I wish he were my brother. He couldn't be, could he? Even if he could only be my cousin, I should like it."

Mrs. Hardy looked at Rock, who laughed and said, "That is more likely than the other."

"I don't see how," said Dimple.

"You will see," said Rock. But at a look from his mother he was silent.

Amy E. Blanchard

They leaned back on the soft cushions, breathing the sweet air, spicy with the scent of the pines through which they were driving.

At Big Run they all begged to get out, to see if there were any fish in the water. They clambered about on the bank and over the stones, till Mrs. Hardy told them it was too late to stop longer, and they drove toward town.

After they had reached the house where Rock and his mother were boarding, they took off their hats and were ready for tea. They wondered if they were all to sit with Mrs. Brisk's family at the table, and dreaded it a little. However, when Rock said, "Come this way, girls," they were a little mystified, for he took them out into the garden.

Under a trellised summerhouse there was set a little table for three, and on the bench a very small table with two little chairs.

"That is for the dolls," explained Rock.

"Oh, Rock!" exclaimed the girls. "Where did they come from? Did you make them?"

"Yes," said he. "Do you like them?"

"They are perfect," said Florence. "Dimple, do see how nicely Celestine sits up to the table."

"And Rubina, too," said Dimple, as she took off her doll's hat. "Don't they look lovely? Look, Rock. What a boy you are."

Rock laughed, and they turned to their own table, which had a tiny bouquet by each plate and a pyramid of fruit in the centre.

The long drive had given them all an appetite, and they did full justice to the croquettes, muffins and fried potatoes before they thought of the jelly, fruit and cake.

"How will we get our chairs and table home?" said Florence.

"I will take them to-morrow," said Rock.

"Oh, no," said Dimple. "It was enough for you to make them, without taking them home, too."

"Well," said Rock, "if the cabinetmaker can't take home his own goods, I think it is a pity."

The girls laughed, and so the matter rested.

"What shall we do now?" asked Rock. "Will you look at pictures, or play games, or what?"

Dimple looked at Florence, and Florence looked at Dimple.

"I think pictures are nice in winter, when you can't be out of doors," said Florence, who never could get enough of out of doors.

So they concluded to play out of doors.

"What nice long grass this is," said Dimple. "We could almost hide ourselves. We might play we were rabbits, and hop about and make nests."

"Let's hide ourselves," cried Florence. "I speak for first count.

"Onery Twoery,
Dickery Day,
Illava, Lullava,
Lackava Lay,
One condemn the American line.
Umny Bumny,
Twenty-nine.
Fillason, Folloson,
Nicholas John.
Queevy, Quavy,

English Navy,
Signum, Sangnum,
Buck!"

"You're out," she sang out to Rock and then went again
rapidly over the count, making herself "It."

Then Dimple and Rock stole softly off to hide themselves,
while Florence covered her eyes by a tree.

"Whoop!" called Dimple, presently.

"Whoop!" called Rock, a moment later.

And Florence went in search of them, but before she found
them, she discovered something else and called out:

"Rock! Dimple! Come here, quick. I have found something so
funny and cunning."

Out of their nests started the children to see Florence standing
over another nest in a trellis, in which was a family of little
baby wrens, opening their small beaks and clamoring to be fed.

"Sh! Sh!" Dimple said, softly. "Don't let's scare them, poor
little things. See, there is the mother bird. She is distressed
because we have found her babies. Oh Rock, don't let any one
else know they are here, for they might hurt them."

"Let us go away now," said Rock, in a whisper. "The poor
mother bird is flying around, and is so troubled. She doesn't
know that we wouldn't harm her little ones for anything." So
they tiptoed away and left the mother in possession.

"What kind of bird was it?" Florence asked, in a low voice.

"Why, don't you know? That was Jenny Wren," returned
Dimple, more accustomed to creatures of woods and fields.

"Was it really Jenny Wren?" exclaimed Florence, delightedly. "I'm so glad I've seen her."

"Didn't you ever see her before? You have heard Mr. Wren sing, haven't you? Oh, how he sings! I think house-wrens are such dear, dear birds. We always put up boxes and cans and such things for them, for we like to have them around, and they can build their nests in quite small places. The other big birds try to drive them away sometimes, but we always try to protect them. Mamma says Jenny Wren is a very neat house-keeper, and takes excellent care of her family. They are such friendly little birds. I love them better than any others."

"Do you believe you have any wrens' nests near the house, this year?" Florence asked.

"Yes, indeed, ever so many. I know just where to look for them. I'll show you some to-morrow. There's one in the funniest place. You know where the bamboo shade is rolled up at the side of the front porch: well, in one end of that a wren has built a nest, and mamma will not have the shade let down till the little birds are ready to fly."

Florence gave a sigh of content. She enjoyed such things so heartily, and saw none of them in her city home.

"I like the robins," put in Rock, "they are such cheerful fellows. Listen to that one whistle. Doesn't it remind you of juicy cherries?"

Dimple laughed. "Yes, and don't they love cherries! I believe they eat half on our trees, and they always pick out the very finest ones."

"Of course. So would you, if you were a robin," Rock returned. "Speaking of birds, Florence, have you ever watched the swallows—the chimney swifts—come home? It's a sight."

"No, I never saw them. Are there any here?" returned Florence, eagerly.

"Lots of them. They build in that old chimney, and they come every year on a certain day of the month. They seem to have a sort of system in the way they circle around, and go down the chimney; just as if they were regularly drilled for it. It's about time for them now. Suppose we sit here and watch them."

This they did, and when the last belated swallow had dropped down into the tall old chimney, they went up to the house where Mrs. Hardy was waiting for them, and where they were glad to listen to her tales of California; its big trees, its fine fruits, and the lovely flowers that grow wild there; and she told many funny tales of the Chinese, till Mr. Dallas made his appearance, and with regretful good-byes they took their leave.

All this time the girls had not once remembered Bubbles. They were having such a good time, and it was not till they were on their way home, when Mr. Dallas questioned them, that they thought of how they had left her on the roof.

"Mrs. Hardy is just lovely, mamma," said Dimple, when they reached home. "I hope she liked me, for I liked her, and, oh mamma! I am so sorry about Bubbles."

"I am glad you like Mrs. Hardy," said her mother, "but the next time Bubbles does wrong, I hope you will tell me, and not punish her yourself. You must remember that she is only a little ignorant, colored girl, and that it is no wonder she wants what you have, for you have played with her, and been with her so much. Of course it was wrong for her to take anything without leave. Were you and Florence good girls?"

"Yes, I think so. Mamma, what did Rock mean when he said he was more likely to be my cousin than my brother?"

"Did he say that?" said Mrs. Dallas, smiling. "Well, so you are."

"Mamma, I don't understand."

"No. I know you don't. You will in a few days. Now go to bed."

"Florence," said Dimple, after they were in bed. "There is another secret somewhere, and I cannot puzzle it out. Mamma wants Mrs. Hardy to be fond of me, and Rock is likely to be my cousin, and all that."

"I can't imagine," answered Florence, sleepily.

"I don't see into it," said Dimple, after thinking a while. "Florence, are you asleep?"

But Florence made no answer, having by that time arrived in dreamland, and Dimple soon followed her, dreaming that she was feeding the little wrens on croquettes, and was taking her doll to drive in California, when a big tree came up to her, and insisted on shaking hands, because it said it was her cousin. She laughed right out in her sleep, and frightened a little mouse back into its hole.

*　*　*　*　*

When the two little girls ran down to breakfast the next morning, they wore very happy faces, for Dimple had just discovered that her birthday was only a week off, and she and Florence had been planning for it.

"Papa always does something very specially nice for me," Dimple had just announced, "and I always have a lovely birthday-cake with icing and candles. Mamma makes it herself, because I always think it tastes better when she does. And she lets me choose what we are to have for dinner. You tell what you like best, Florence, and we'll have that."

"I like fried chicken better than anything, except, of course, ice cream and cake."

　　　　　Amy E. Blanchard

"So do I. I'm so glad you like what I do, and I'm very glad my birthday is in June, for it is such a rosy month, and we can have strawberries with the ice cream. There are so many good things to eat in June; strawberries, and peas, and asparagus and—oh, I don't know what all." This conversation took place before breakfast, and Dimple was sitting on the floor hugging her knees, and looking as contented as it was possible to be.

They were still talking on the important subject when they entered the dining-room.

"What's all this about birthdays?" asked Mr. Dallas, looking up from his morning paper.

"Why, papa, don't you know my birthday will be next week?" returned Dimple, as she went up to give him his morning kiss. "Aren't you glad?" she added.

"Is it an occasion for great joyfulness? I'm not so sure of that. Don't you know it makes mamma feel very serious to have a daughter eight—or is it nine—years old? And as for myself, I begin to feel the grey hairs popping out all over my head at the very thought of it."

"I shall be nine years old. But, papa, you are always making out that you are old and that makes me feel sorry. I don't see a single grey hair. People are not very old till they are forty, at least, are they?"

"Well, no, but they are rather decrepit when they reach such extreme old age as that—Uncle Heath is forty you know, and see what a tottering old man he is."

"Now, papa, you are laughing at me. I don't believe you'll have grey hairs for years and years."

"They are starting, I am sure. However, we'll change the subject, if you wish. What do you expect me to give you on that festal day? Not another doll, surely?"

"No—I don't know—perhaps."

"Oh, you are insatiable as to dolls. I believe if any one were to give you a dozen at Christmas you would be glad to have a dozen more on New Years. I don't believe Florence is so doll-crazy."

"Yes, she is. Aren't you, Florence?"

Florence nodded.

"Nevertheless," continued Mr. Dallas, "I'll promise no doll this time. Shall it be books? Perhaps we'd better consult mamma. Come to think of it, I had an idea about this same birthday. It seems to me I thought it wouldn't be a bad plan to provide some amusement for rainy days."

The two little girls looked at each other, and Dimple hung her head.

"What do you think?" Mr. Dallas asked, quizzically. "It seems to me that I have heard that the rain produces a singularly bad effect upon two little girls I know."

"Yes, papa, we were horrid, especially one time. We didn't know what to do, and so—and so—"

   'Satan found some mischief still
   For idle hands to do;'

was that the way of it?"

Dimple glanced at Florence shamefacedly. "Yes, papa, I'm afraid it was just that way," she replied, meekly.

"Well, as I said before, I think it wouldn't be a bad plan to provide against such trouble. Perhaps that birthday will show you a way out of future difficulty."

Amy E. Blanchard

And so it proved, for on her birthday morning the secret of the little house was revealed.

"You must wait till after breakfast to see your birthday gifts, daughter," Mrs. Dallas said, as Dimple came bounding into the room to receive her nine kisses.

"Oh, mamma, why? I always have them the first thing. Do tell me where they are. Downstairs or up here?"

"Downstairs, in one sense, but they are not in the house at all."

Dimple's eyes opened wide. "Not in the house? Florence, just listen. There is a great secret. Oh, dear, how can I wait?"

"Well, dearie," returned her mother, "the sooner you are dressed the sooner the secret will come. See, I am nearly ready to go down."

"Please help me, just this morning, mamma. It will make it so much easier, and it's my birthday, you know."

"Very well, since you are the person of importance to-day, I will help you."

"Hurry up, Florence," cried Dimple. "Come in here and I'll fasten your buttons while mamma does mine; then we'll get through all the sooner."

Although Dimple, the day before, had carefully selected the day's bill of fare, the breakfast was scarcely tasted, her favorite waffles offering no inducement for her to linger over them, so great was her excitement, and she watched eagerly till her father pushed back his chair, and declared himself ready for orders. It seemed to Dimple that he had never had such an appetite before, and she watched with anxious interest as he helped himself to waffles from each plateful that Bubbles brought in. There was a twinkle in his eyes as Dimple at last heaved a long sigh, and he immediately arose and led the way through the garden to the little new house between the house and the stable.

"We'll look in here," he remarked, as he unlocked the door.

Although Dimple had been quite curious to see the inside of the "house for little chicks," she was rather disappointed at the delay, for she thought, perhaps, her papa had something for her in the stable, a fox terrier, or maybe a goat, since she had expressed a wish for both. But when the door of the little house was opened her surprise was so great that she gave expression to one long-drawn "Oh-h!" and looked from one to the other half bewildered.

For, instead of a brooder and an "inkybator," she saw before her the dearest little room with white curtains at the window, a rug upon the floor, a small cooking stove in one corner, a table, chairs, and all to suit a little girl. Upon the shelves were ranged plates, cups, saucers and dishes, and a cupboard in the corner looked as if it might hold other necessary things for housekeeping. Moreover, her family of dolls sat along in a row on the window-seat, looking as expectant as is the nature of dolls to look.

"Well, Dot, how do you like it?" asked Mr. Dallas, smiling down at the child whose color came and went in her fair little face.

"Oh, papa! Oh, papa! is it truly my house?" she asked, clasping him closely.

"Yes, it is truly yours. I thought a rainy day house might help to keep our little chicks out of mischief, because here they can peep as loud as they choose and it will not disturb any one."

"You said it was for little chicks, and I never once thought you meant us. Did you, Florence? It is lovely, lovely. Oh, papa, you are too good."

"I think it is a matter of self-defence, for if you and Florence are so ambitious as to take violent possession of your neighbors' houses, it seemed to me there would be no end of complaints, and the best way to prevent further housebreaking was to give you a house where you could cook and sweep and exercise your domestic tastes to your hearts' content."

Dimple understood all this banter, and she laughingly said, "Florence, we are like the birds that try to take the wrens' houses to live in. But now we have a nest of our own we won't do it any more, papa. Thank you so much. It is the most lovely surprise I ever had in all my life."

"I'm glad you like your house, Mistress Eleanor Dallas; but, dear me, I can't stand here chattering. I must be off."

Dimple gave him an ecstatic parting hug, and returned to a survey of her house.

"Papa gives you the house, and I the furniture," her mother told her. "You must try to keep the place neat and clean. Of course, Bubbles can help you, sometimes, but I want you to learn to take care of it yourself and to be a good housekeeper."

"Like Jenny Wren. Oh, yes, mamma, I will try. Florence, we'll put up boxes for the wrens, up there by the door, and maybe they will come and build. Mamma, may we have our ice cream and cake out here this afternoon?"

"Yes, if you like, and you may go over and ask Rock Hardy to come, and Leila and Eugene Clark too, if you like to have them. That will make quite a nice little party. You can use your own dishes, and have all the fun you choose."

"Won't that be fine!" cried Dimple, softly clapping her hands. "Shall we go now?" she asked.

"Yes, unless you would rather wait."

"No, I'd rather go now, so I won't have to think about it, for I shall not want to leave my house to-day; it is so dear and cunning. And, Florence, when we come back, we'll gather some flowers and make everything look as pretty as possible. Just think, we'll be like grown-up ladies, with a house, and a servant, and—oh, mamma, please let Bubbles wear a cap."

Mrs. Dallas laughed. "I don't believe we will insist upon that, but you can rig up one for her if you like, when she is out here. Now I must go in."

"Come, Florence, we'll go and invite the company, and get that over with, and then we'll have nothing to interrupt us the rest of the day," said Dimple. "Won't it be fine to come out here on rainy days and make all the noise we want. What time shall we tell the children to come?" she called after her mother, who was just stepping off the little porch.

"At four o'clock, I think."

"That's the time Rock had his tea-party," said Dimple. "I am glad we can invite him to our feast, because we had such a nice time over there. I wonder if he knows anything about this being our little house. If he doesn't, won't he be surprised!"

It proved that Rock didn't know, and he was as interested as any one could wish;—so much so, indeed, that he begged to go over at once to see it, and his mother allowed him to do so.

"My! but it's fine," he declared, examining both outside and in. "You might have a pretty little garden out here, and plant some vines to grow over the porch."

"So we might," Dimple responded, "I never thought of that. It will make the little porch so much prettier. Just think, I never dreamed that it was being built for me."

"Your father is awfully good," returned Rock, adding soberly, "I hope it runs in the family."

Dimple laughed, but looked sober herself, immediately after. "I'm afraid I'll never be as good as papa and mamma, for I do horrid things," she said. She looked at Florence wistfully, then lifted one of her cousin's soft auburn curls, and laid her cheek against it; to which Florence responded by giving her a sudden kiss. They both remembered that day in the garret.

Rock became so interested in the idea of a garden, that, after Mrs. Dallas's consent was gained, he spent most of the day in digging up a little patch in which the children planted a remarkable collection of plants, both wild and cultivated. They even put in some corn, so as to have roasting ears, Dimple said, and a pumpkin seed, because she liked pumpkin pies.

They were so busy all day that they were scarcely willing to go in to prepare for their feast.

Leila and Eugene Clark were properly impressed with the new house; yet, with the others, were quite ready to stop their play that they might do justice to the big cake with its nine candles, and its wreath of flowers; while the amount of ice cream eaten showed plainly that the refreshments were quite to the taste of the guests. Leila brought Dimple a box of candy, and Eugene presented her with a bunch of beautiful roses. Rock, too, although he hardly could spare the time to rush home and get his gift for her, had something to donate; an exquisite little fan with carved ivory sticks, that he said was made in China, and which his mother had bought in California. Mrs. Hardy added to the gift a dainty pink sash, and Florence had struggled in secret to make Rubina a new frock, and had succeeded very well. So Dimple felt herself bountifully remembered.

"It's been just the very happiest day I ever had," said the little girl as she stood in her white night gown, ready for bed.

"I ought to be a very, very good girl, mamma; and I have done so many naughty things lately, but I didn't think."

"Didn't Think is a bad enemy to most little girls," said Mrs.

Dallas, holding her daughter's fair head against her shoulder.

"Did *you* have to fight him?"

"I did, indeed."

"That's a comfort. Perhaps when I grow up, I may be a little weeny, weeny bit like you, darling mamsey. Please give me nine more kisses."

"One on your forehead; one on each cheek; one on each eyelid; one between the eyes; one on your chin; one on your mouth, and where shall I put the other?"

"Here, in the tickley place under my chin. Now say 'my blessed child'; that always makes me feel good, and then I'll pop into bed."

But the head was no sooner on the pillow than it was bobbed up again, and there came the whisper, "Mamma, please kiss Florence more than one time, and call her something nice." And when this was done, two very tired, but very happy, little girls kissed each other, and in a few moments were fast asleep.

CHAPTER VII

HOUSEKEEPERS

"Mamma," said Dimple, with her elbows on the arm of her mother's chair, "what are you thinking about so hard? You have a little puckery frown between your eyes, whenever you look at Florence and me. What have we been doing?"

"Nothing," replied Mrs. Dallas, smiling. "I was wondering if it would be wise to leave you two alone here with Bubbles for a day. Mrs. Hardy wants me to go to the city with her to-morrow, and I promised Sylvy some time ago that she should have the day; she wants to go off on an excursion, and has been making great preparations. I could not have the heart to disappoint her, and your papa will not be at home for another week, so I am very doubtful about leaving you."

"Oh! do go, mamma," cried Dimple, clapping her hands. "We can keep house beautifully, can't we, Florence?—and it will be such fun. Do go, there's a darling. We'll be just as grown-up as possible, and do anything you tell us."

"And you will not be afraid?"

"Not in the least. We'll have Bubbles, you know, and she can run awfully fast, if we get ill, and want the doctor," replied Dimple, cheerfully.

"I hope no such effort will be needed on Bubbles' part. You

must not turn the house upside down, nor empty all the trunks and chests upon the floor of the attic."

"Now, mamma," exclaimed Dimple, reproachfully, "why do you remind us of that?"

Mrs. Dallas laughed at the woe-begone tone.

"That you may remember not to do it again," she replied; then she added, "Well, I'll think about it a little longer. I promised to let Mrs. Hardy know this afternoon. Now run along and let me think."

"You will tell us as soon as you make up your mind," said Dimple, as she left the room with Florence.

"Yes, yes; don't keep me any longer from my 'think.'"

"Don't you hope she will go?" asked Florence. "I think it would be lots of fun to have the house all to ourselves for a whole day. What shall we do, Dimple?"

"Oh, there will be lots to do," replied Dimple, importantly. "There will be the beds to make, and the house to put in order, and dinner to get. Oh, Florence! What shall we have for dinner? What should you like?"

"I don't know, exactly; baked custards are nice."

"Yes," assented Dimple, doubtfully, "but I'm afraid we couldn't manage to make them just right; they seem sort of hard; and you don't like huckleberry pudding."

"Then let's have apple 'cobbler;' we both like that."

"Yes, and it is easy, at least I think it is, just crust and apples. Well, we'll have that. I do wish mamma would hurry up and tell us."

The two established themselves on the lowest step, as near as possible to the library, where Mrs. Dallas was sitting.

"Don't make such a noise," said Dimple, as Florence, to while away the time, began to sing; "you will keep mamma from thinking. Just let's whisper." So for a half hour or more a little whispering sound went on, interspersed by stifled laughter. Then at the noise of Mrs. Dallas' hand upon the door knob, the two girls sprang to their feet.

"Hurry up, mamma, tell us," cried Dimple, as the door opened.

"When you give me a chance," replied Mrs. Dallas, smiling. "I am going. Does that please you?"

"Oh! oh!" cried the two, dancing up and down.

"How flattering you are," said Mrs. Dallas, laughing; "I never had pleasure so fully shown for such a cause. So you will be delighted to get rid of me?"

"Now mamma! Now auntie!" came in chorus. "It isn't that at all, but it will be such fun, and we are going to make an 'apple cobbler' for dinner."

"Are you! Who said so?"

"Why, mayn't we?" asked Dimple, somewhat taken aback.

"Who will make it?"

"Why, we will, of course. I've seen Sylvy do it often, and I know exactly how. Do, do let us, mamma."

It seemed too bad to dampen their ardor, and Mrs. Dallas, rather dubiously, consented, but charged them not to eat under cooked dough, or raw apples.

Every one was up betimes the next morning. Sylvy had set everything in readiness for breakfast, and had taken an early departure, and Mrs. Dallas was to leave on the nine o'clock train.

"I shall be back by eight o'clock," she told the children. "Don't set the house afire, and don't make yourselves ill."

"Now, don't worry over us," said Dimple, loftily; "we shall do finely."

But she did feel a little sinking of heart as her mamma's form was lost to view, and the two girls turned from the gate.

"I wish Rock were not going with them," remarked Dimple. "It would be nice to have him here."

"I don't think it would," replied Florence; "we'd have to entertain him, and maybe he doesn't like 'apple cobbler.'"

"That is true," returned Dimple, her spirits rising at the suggestion of some active employment. "Now let us go and make the beds, while Bubbles does the dishes." And they set to work, with much chattering, to follow out this duty.

"There, now, it looks as neat as possible," pronounced Dimple, as she closed the shutters to keep out the glaring sun. "Just hang up that towel that has fallen down, Florence, and then we'll go downstairs and shut up the rest of the house; by that time Bubbles will be through her work, and we can all play till it is time to get dinner."

Bubbles had just emptied her dish-pan and was about to scour the knives when they entered the kitchen.

"Hurry up, Bubbles," said Dimple, "so we can all go out and play. We want you to take care of Celestine and Rubina, while we go out shopping. Mamma said we might use the pieces in this," holding out a calico bag. "That is, we are just going to roll them up and have them for dry goods. The dry goods shop is to be at the end of the porch, where the bench is. We have cut out a great big newspaper man to sell the goods. We'll have to pin him against the railing, Florence, or he won't stand up, he is so limp. Isn't he fine and tall? His name is Mr. Star, because we cut him out of the *Evening Star.*"

Their play proved to be so very interesting that it was after twelve o'clock before the little housekeepers remembered that they had a dinner to prepare, and that the making and baking of their apple pie would take some time. Then it appeared that Bubbles, in her haste to join the play, had forgotten the fire, which was nearly out.

"Never mind, we'll put in some wood," concluded Dimple, cheerfully. "I've seen Sylvy do it lots of times, to hurry up the oven. Run, Bubbles, and get some wood. Then you can pare the apples, while I make the crust."

"Let me pare the apples," suggested Florence; "it is such fun to put them on that little thing and turn the crank, while the skin comes off so easily."

"Well, you do that," agreed Dimple. "And Bubbles can set the table."

"Why doesn't this apple go right?" said Florence. "It wabbles around so and—there!—it has gone bouncing off to the other side of the kitchen; how provoking!"

"It is a sort of 'skew-jawed' one," pronounced Dimple. "I can never do anything with those on the parer. Pick out the ones that are perfectly round and smooth, and they will go all right. I wonder how much shortening I ought to put in. Does that look like enough to you?"

Florence viewed the pan critically. "I don't know," she replied, doubtfully. "I don't believe I know much about it; it looks like a pretty big lump."

"Oh, I'll call it enough," decided Dimple. "There, it is ready to roll out. Somehow, it doesn't roll very easily."

"Let me try," offered Florence, who, having finished paring the apples, was watching her cousin.

"It is not easy," she said, after banging away with the rolling-pin. "Maybe Bubbles can do it; her arms are stronger;" and, after this third effort, some sort of crust was ready, with which to line the pan.

"It seems pretty thick," Dimple declared, looking at it with a dissatisfied eye; "but it is the best we can do."

"Oh, it will taste all right," encouraged Florence. "Now for the apples; what else, Dimple?"

"Sugar, and little bits of butter and—what else? Oh, yes, a little sprinkling of flour. Now the top goes on, and it can go into the oven. I wonder how long it will take to bake. It is one o'clock, and I am beginning to get hungry.

"The oven isn't very hot," she presently pronounced. "Put some more wood in, Bubbles. Oh, what is the matter, Florence?" as an exclamation made her turn in her cousin's direction.

"I have burned my hand," said Florence, trying hard not to cry. "I wanted to look at the fire, and when I lifted the lid, the steam from the kettle came just where I put my hand. I didn't know steam could burn so."

"It is worse than anything else," informed Dimple. "It is too bad. I'll get something to put on it, to take the burn out."

"Kar'sene's mighty good," suggested Bubbles.

"Yes, and so is flour; and linseed oil is good; that will be the best," and the bottle being brought, the wounded hand was bound up and Florence retired from action and sat on the step watching the others, while she nursed her hurt.

"Let me see," went on Dimple, bustling about. "We have chicken, and bread and butter, and sliced tomatoes, and milk, and the 'cobbler.' It is doing, Florence; it is beginning to brown."

"I wish it would hurry up," Florence said. "I'm hungry, and, oh! how my hand hurts."

"Isn't it any better?"

"A little; but it doesn't feel a bit good."

"It is too bad," said Dimple, sympathetically, coming over and putting a floury hand on her cousin's.

"I smell the pie," she exclaimed, jumping up. "It must be burning," and she ran to the oven.

"Is it burned?" asked Florence, anxiously.

"No, only just a weeny bit caught. I'll take it out. Doesn't it look good?"

Florence gave an admiring assent, and they proceeded to take their meal; but alas!—when the pie was cut a mass of sticky dough and raw apple was disclosed to the disappointment of them all.

"We'll have to put it back and eat it after awhile," said Florence. "It will taste just as good then."

"Yes, and we can eat cake for dessert," and the pie was again placed in the oven.

Not long after, a rapping was heard at the side porch. "Who in the world can that be around there!" exclaimed Dimple. "Go and see, Bubbles."

Bubbles looked out, cautiously, for it was not the usual place for any one to make an appearance. Presently she came back with big eyes and a somewhat scared expression. "Hit's a man, Miss Dimple," she said, in an excited whisper, "with a gre't big haid an' long hair, an' somethin' on his back."

Florence and Dimple looked at each other. "Let's peep and see," whispered the latter, as the rapping, which had ceased, began again.

They peeped timidly through the shutters. "He looks queer," said Dimple, "maybe he is crazy."

"Oh!" cried Florence, with a stifled scream, "maybe he is an escaped lunatic. Dimple, let's lock all the doors, and hide," and the two ran into the kitchen, barring and locking the door, and then raced upstairs as fast as they could go, with Bubbles close following at their heels.

Florence buried her face in the pillows and covered up her head with the bed clothes; Bubbles crawled under the bed, then, as the rapping continued louder than before, interspersed with calls of "Hey, there! Hey, there!" Dimple, feeling very brave, opened the window and cried out, "Go away!" then she shut down the window with a slam, and sprang into the middle of the room with very red cheeks and a beating heart.

After a little time all was quiet, and the three timidly ventured downstairs to find the pie baked to such a crisp brownness, that it barely escaped being called black. It was set aside to cool, and after a short parley, the children set out to reconnoitre, armed with such weapons as they thought most useful. Bubbles carried an axe, Florence a bottle of ammonia, which she meant to throw in the face of the intruder "to take his breath away," she declared; and Dimple bore a long rope and a pair of large scissors. She intended, she said, to snip at the man if he came near her, and, when he was overpowered

Amy E. Blanchard

by Florence's ammonia, to bind him hand and foot with the rope.

But, after a long and thorough search, no one was found about the premises, and they all returned to the house to eat the "cobbler," which by this time was cool.

"It doesn't taste like Sylvy's," said Dimple. "I believe I forgot to put any salt in the crust, and where it isn't hard it is tough; there! I didn't put any water in it, of course there is scarcely any juice. I was going to save some for mamma, but I don't think I shall. We'll give it away to the first person we can," she continued to Florence.

This happened to be an organ grinder, who made his appearance at the gate. Bubbles was despatched with the message that they hadn't any money, but there was some pie, and the organ grinder departed, whether grateful or not, they did not learn.

"It seems to me it has been a pretty long day," said Dimple, as the afternoon wore on. "Five o'clock. Three hours before we can possibly expect mamma. I should think she would get dreadfully tired of housekeeping," she continued, remembering her discouraging pie. "I don't feel as if I wanted any supper, do you, Florence?"

"Not now," replied Florence; "but your mamma will want some."

"Oh, well, Bubbles can attend to it," decided Dimple. "I'm tired of seeing dishes and dabs. What shall we do next, Florence?"

"We haven't cleared up the porch yet. Mr. Star is out there and all the pieces."

"Sure enough. Well, we'll get those put away, and then we can dress. I wonder what became of the crazy man."

"Why do you remind me of him?" said Florence, plaintively. "I had almost forgotten, and now I shall dream of him."

"I don't believe he was crazy," said Dimple. "I suppose he had something to sell. I thought so at the time, but I began, to get scared and couldn't stop. Roll up Mr. Star, Florence, we may want him again. There! I have the bag and all the rest of the things. You bring Mr. Star and the dolls."

Just here came a "Hallo!" from around the corner of the house. The children gave a suppressed scream which changed into a hearty laugh when Rock appeared; and with words tumbling over each other they began to give a breathless recital of the day's experiences which amused Rock vastly.

"But how did you happen to be here?" the girls remembered at last to ask. "We thought you had gone to the city."

"No, I didn't go after all. Mr. Brisk was going off in the country, and mamma gave me my choice of places, so I thought I'd not enjoy going shopping very much, and I decided to go with Mr. Brisk. We got back about half an hour ago, and I came over to see if you wouldn't go back to the house with me. I want to show you something I found."

"What is it?"

"Wait till you see."

"I'm afraid we oughtn't to leave the house," said Dimple.

"Can't you lock it up? We won't be gone long, and I'll come back and stay with you till your mother comes. Then I can walk home with my mother, for she'll stop here first."

"That will be very nice, but I don't believe we dare lock it up."

"Let Bubbles stay."

Amy E. Blanchard

But Bubbles' eyes nearly popped out of her head at this suggestion; and, finally, after many plans Rock went over to the house of the man whom Mr. Dallas employed to take care of the garden and stable, and he promised to stay on the place to give Bubbles countenance, till the others should return.

"I've got a job over there, anyhow," he said, "though I mostly leaves about this time, but I can do what I have to do as well now as in the morning." Therefore the children felt perfectly safe in leaving Bubbles.

Rock led the way to Mr. Brisk's workhouse. "What I've to show you is in here," he said. The girls followed him somewhat timidly, but were reassured when Rock drew out a box of shavings where, cuddled up, they saw a cat and three little bits of kittens.

"Oh! how cunning," cried Dimple, getting down on her knees. "You little tootsy-wootsy, deary things. Aren't they soft? Oh! if we might have them. There are three, just one a piece. Rock, don't you believe we might have them?"

"We'll go and ask," said Rock, and they ran pell-mell into the house.

"What is the matter?" said Mr. Brisk, starting up lest something were wrong.

"We are only going to ask Mrs. Brisk if we may have the kittens," they cried, breathlessly.

Mrs. Brisk was standing in the hall, and heard their story.

"Well! Well! Well!" she said. "If old Topple hasn't another lot of kittens. Have them? To be sure you may, and welcome, when they are big enough to take from their mother."

The girls clapped their hands delightedly and went back to the little blind things, who, with their tight shut eyes, were mewing and nosing against each other.

"Now let's choose," said Rock, after they had taken them out on the grass where it was lighter. "Two black, and one black and white. If you girls like the black ones best I'll take the other, or if either of you like that best, I'll take one of the black ones."

So, after much talking, Dimple chose a black one, and Florence the black and white, while Rock expressed himself delighted with the other black one as really what he liked the best.

"I shall name mine Jet," said he.

"And mine I'll name Onyx, and call it Nyxy for short," said Dimple.

"And mine shall be Marble," said Florence.

So that question being decided they left them, "like birds in their nest," said Dimple, and started for home, for it was growing late.

"We couldn't carry the kittens home to-night, anyhow," said Florence; "but I do hope we can see them often, and that I can take mine home."

She did take it home, and it grew to be a big cat; though before she went, the children often laughed to see Rock coming in with the three little things in a basket, bringing them over for a visit. He did this several times, taking them back to their mother, until one day they came to stay.

Although time dragged, eight o'clock did come at last, and the hour brought Mrs. Dallas.

"And you are really glad to have me back again," she said, with an arm around each little girl, "though you were so glad to

Amy E. Blanchard

have me go. And how did the pie turn out?"

"It wasn't good," admitted Dimple, candidly; "so we gave it to an organ-grinder."

"What charitable, generous children, to be sure," laughed Mrs. Dallas. "By the way, Dimple, I forgot to tell you that possibly the paperhanger might be here; he was to come one day this week to paper the upper hall."

Dimple looked at Florence and Florence looked at Dimple. "We thought he was a crazy man," presently said the latter, in a shamefaced way.

"Crazy! Why, what do you mean?"

"He came to the side door," explained Dimple. "Those were rolls of paper on his back, Florence, and we got frightened and wouldn't let him in."

"You silly little geese! I see I must not leave you again."

"But everything else was all right," Florence informed her, "only I burned my hand a little. I had almost forgotten it, Dimple."

"Then you don't want me to go away, altogether," said Mrs. Dallas.

"No indeed," said they both, in the most emphatic manner.

"You dearest, loveliest," continued Dimple; "it is too delicious to see you again."

"And I didn't dream about the crazy man after all," said Florence, the next morning.

CHAPTER VIII

ADRIFT

During this time Mr. Atkinson was not forgotten, and the two little girls spent many a happy morning in his beautiful garden, for even the small house which Mr. Dallas had built for Dimple, was not proof against the attractions Mr. Atkinson's place had to offer. They were careful not to venture beyond bounds, and kept in the walks and on the porches, but one hot day they wandered down to where a fence marked the limits of the place in that direction. Then came a steep bank sloping down to Big Run which, a little further on, emptied into the river.

It was a wild, romantic spot and full of charm for the two little girls whose fancies pictured all sorts of possible things. The hollows, in the scraggy willows bending over the stream, might be the hiding-places of nymphs or fairies; yonder soft sward dotted with buttercups and daisies, might be the favorite spot for a midnight revel; among those rocks queer little gnomes might live. Florence was especially struck with it all. She had never been quite so near to such a picturesque spot, and now nothing would do but that they should climb the fence and explore further.

"There isn't a soul anywhere to be seen," said Florence, "and it will be perfectly safe."

"Suppose we should meet a fierce dog," Dimple, a little more cautious, suggested.

"Oh, no, we're not likely to at all. Dogs are not going to such a place as that, at least, I don't think so. It would be perfectly fine to go out on one of those willow trees, and hang our feet over the water."

"Suppose we should slip and fall in."

"Oh, we'll be careful; besides the branches of the trees hang so far over the stream that we couldn't fall very far, anyhow, and it is very shallow there. We'll only get a wetting and it's such a hot day I shouldn't mind if we did. If we should sit there very quietly we might see fairies."

"Do you believe there are fairies, really?"

"Why, yes,—I'm not sure. There may be, you know. Wouldn't it be funny to see a tiny little being, in a red cloak or a spun-silver robe, come out from the hollow of a tree and say, 'Maiden, your wish shall be granted'?"

"What wish?"

"Any wish we happen to be making at the time. Come on, Dimple, I am just crazy to go." And Florence put her foot on the fence and was soon over, Dimple following.

It was not so easy as it seemed, to get out on the trees, and they decided not to attempt it, but thought they would wander along the brink of the stream, and in doing this they discovered all sorts of wonderful things in what Florence called the Fairy Dell: moss-grown rocks from which sprung tiny bell-shaped flowers; a circle of wee pink toadstools, which indeed seemed fit for the elfin folk; a wild grapevine with a most delightfully arranged swing on which the two girls "teetered" away in great joy; shining pebbles, bits of rose-colored quartz, a forest of plumy ferns, and all such like things, over which the city child exclaimed and marveled.

At last they were obliged to cross a little bridge, for the bank became higher and higher on that side, and a little further walking showed them the river.

"Oh!" Florence exclaimed. "Isn't this fine? I wish we could go out rowing. See those girls over there by that funny flat sort of boat. They are going to get on it. Come, let us go down and watch them."

They clambered down and were soon on the brink of the river. Two or three girls, much older than Dimple and Florence, were pulling a small flat barge up on the sands. One of the girls recognized Dimple. "Hallo, Eleanor," she cried. "Where did you come from? Don't you want to get on with us?"

"Oh, do let us," whispered Florence.

"Are you going out on the river?" asked Dimple.

"No, we are only going to get on this flat boat, and sit here where we can get the breeze, and maybe we will fish. We brought some tackle along with us. Come, give me your hand. There, you are landed. Come, little girl, there is plenty of room." She held out her hand to Florence, who eagerly accepted the invitation, and was soon by her cousin's side.

"Isn't it nice?" said Dimple.

"Fine," Florence responded, heartily, as she sat down in the bottom of the boat.

"It's rather sunny, though," Dimple remarked.

"Oh, you mustn't mind that. We're going to fish. Don't you want to try your luck?"

Dimple looked rather disgustedly at the can of angle-worms and decided that she would look on.

Amy E. Blanchard

"What are you going to do, Libbie?" Dimple's acquaintance inquired of one of the other girls.

"I'm going to try to get the boat out where it will float. It's such fun to have it bob up and down," replied the girl addressed. She had a long pole and was pushing the boat off from the shore. It was fastened to a stake, so it could only career around a little, and Dimple's friend Callie Spear assured the little girls that it was perfectly secure, and so they gave themselves up to their enjoyment.

Both Florence and Dimple felt very proud of being invited to join this company of older girls; and, while the latter amused themselves by fishing, the two little ones set afloat small chips, freighted with the daisies they had gathered, and wondered how far they could go before they should upset.

"Wouldn't it be funny if they sailed all the way to the ocean and were seen by the people on one of the big steamers. They would wonder how in the world the daisy people got out so far." Florence said this as she was watching a chip rapidly drifting down stream. Suddenly she became aware that the shore was further away than she supposed, and she cried, "Oh, how wide the water is! See how far it is to the shore."

The other girls looked up, startled, and to their dismay discovered that their boat had slipped its moorings and was fast drifting down the river, nearer and nearer to the current of midstream. They looked at each other with scared faces, but they did not want to alarm the little girls, and so Callie said, with a forced laugh: "Oh, that's all right. We'll get in easily enough. Some one will see us from the shore, or a boat will come along that can tow us in. It's rather fun to have a little adventure." However, she eagerly scanned the shore and the water; but no help seemed to be near, and the boat was drifting on and on.

Dimple realized that they were moving further and further away from home, as she saw the objects on the shore grow smaller and smaller. The big tears began to gather in her eyes.

"Don't cry, dear," said Callie, soothingly. "We'll get home all right."

"But suppose we shouldn't. Suppose we should drift on and on down to where the steamboats come up, and we should keep going till it got dark, and nobody should see us, and we should get run into and drowned. Oh dear! I want my mamma, and my papa."

Florence took alarm at this, and, putting her head in Dimple's lap, began to cry too.

The older girls were scarcely less frightened, for they knew there was a danger in their reaching the rapids, and in being whirled around between the rocks, when they would be very likely to upset, even in a boat like the one in which they were. They managed, however, to show less fear, in their endeavor to calm the younger children.

"Why, we'll get home long before we reach the steamboats," said Emma Bradford, cheerfully. "Haven't you seen the river in a freshet? And don't you know how it carries all sorts of things along? haystacks, and sheds, and even houses with people in them, I've seen, and they are always rescued."

Libbie Jackson was looking over the side of the boat. "It is very shallow here. We could almost walk ashore," she said.

"We are right over the old ford," said Callie. Suddenly she sprang to her feet and began to tear off the skirt of her frock. As soon as she was freed from it she began to wave it frantically. "I see some one on shore," she exclaimed, excitedly. "All shout as loud as you can, girls;" and across the water rang the shrill cry of "Help! Help! Help!"

The man riding along the shore caught sight of the flapping skirt, of hats waving frantically, and the cry of "help" came faintly to his ears. He stopped his horse and looked around. "Them gals is adrift," he said to himself. "Whatever possessed 'em I don't know, but I reckon I'll have to see if I can't stop 'em."

He rode to the water's edge and looked across. "We're right at the ford," he remarked, as if his horse could understand what he said. "It won't hurt you to go out," he continued. "It's a hot day, and you can get cooled off good." And the girls in the boat were rejoiced to see the horse headed toward them.

"Oh, how lucky that we're at the ford," said Callie, "otherwise the man might not venture. See, Eleanor! See, Florence, he can tow us in. Haul up that bit of rope, girls, while I put on my skirt."

The man was not long in coming alongside. "What happened ye?" he asked. "A lot o' gals like you ain't no business gittin' into such a fix. Whar did ye start from, anyhow? How long ye been driftin'?"

They told him how the trouble had occurred, and he replied with, "Humph! I reckon ye'd better not try that agin. You're a matter o' five mile from home, and the boat don't belong to ye, ye say. How do ye expect to git back? And how are ye going to manage about the boat? Do ye know whose it is?"

"No, but we can find out," said Callie. "What do you think would be the best way to get it home again? Isn't it a dreadful fix to be in? Can you suggest any way to help us?"

"I might take it up for ye to-morrow, maybe, but ye'll have to pay for it."

"How much would you charge us?"

"Lemme see; a couple of dollars."

The girls looked at each other, and held a whispered

consultation whichresulted in Callie's agreeing to the amount, each girl promising to put in her share.

The boat was easily towed to the shore; but here it was wet and slippery, and it required considerable agility to get ashore without slipping in the soft mud. Every one accomplished it safely but Dimple, whose foot slipped, and over she went, full length into the mire. A sorry sight she was indeed, when she was picked up; plastered from head to foot; face, hands and hair full of the soft ooze. But after she had been scraped off, Callie concluded that it would be better to let the sun dry her well, before attempting to get rid of the rest.

"About this job," said the man, "it's worth somethin', ain't it? It's considerable out of my way, travelin' to the middle of the river; besides I've got to look out for that boat, that nobody don't steal it."

"How much do you expect?" asked Callie, meekly. This was getting more and more serious.

"A couple of dollars ain't much when ye consider there's five of ye, and if I hadn't stopped ye, ye'd be goin' yet. My name's Bill Hart, and any one'll tell you I'm safe. Ye needn't be afraid but what I'll bring back the boat."

"Well, if you will come to my house, you shall have your money," said Callie. "Do you know where Mr. Harley Spear lives?"

"Big white house, left side the main street. Yes, I know. You his gal?"

"I'm his daughter."

"All right. I reckon ye can git home now, can't ye? It's a straight road along the river. I must be gettin' on. I'll fetch the boat back to-morrow."

The girls saw him disappear, and stood, a most subdued little group. Dimple felt herself to be in a very unhappy plight, and dreaded meeting any one. How should she get home through the town without being seen? She looked very miserable and woe-begone as she thought of all this.

"Well, girls, we'll have to be up and doing," said Callie. "We've a five mile walk before us, and it's a pretty hot day, so we'll have to take it slowly. You'll have plenty of time to get dried off, before we get there, Eleanor, so don't look so unhappy, you poor little midget. Think how dreadful it is for me who got you into this scrape. I can never forgive myself for it."

"I'll tell you what let's do," said Libbie. "Let Eleanor take off her frock, and we'll wash it out in the river, and dry it as we go along. We're not likely to meet any one, and it's so hot she'll not take cold going without it. We can hold it out between us as we walk along, so it will dry before we get home, and it will be clean at least."

Dimple was so grateful for this suggestion that she could have hugged Libbie; but she did not know her very well, and only expressed her thanks very fervently. At the first opportunity the frock was washed out, and really looked much better. "I wish I could do my stockings, too," said Dimple, "but I couldn't go barefoot. Mamma wouldn't like me to, although I'd like to." So this part of her dress had to remain as it was, and the girls took up their line of march again.

"I am so thirsty I don't know what to do," said Callie. "If I don't have a drink I'll drop by the way. I hate to think of drinking that warm river water; besides, it isn't so easy to get it."

"There's a spring somewhere further along," said Emma Bradford. "If we can manage to exist till we reach it, we can rest there. We shall be half starved, too, by the time we get home."

"If we only had something to eat we could sit down by the spring till it grew cooler, and we'd have a sort of a picnic. Oh, girls, we left all our fishing tackle in the boat! I never once thought of it."

"Nor I."

"Nor I."

"Perhaps Bill What's-his-name will bring it back when he comes with the boat. We've made a pretty expensive trip of it, as it is, without losing our fishing tackle. Think what that four dollars would buy: such a lot of ice cream and soda water," said Callie.

"Don't mention such things when we are consumed with thirst, and are so warm," said Emma.

"We may have to pay for the use of the boat, too," said Libbie. "I suppose we are out at least a dollar apiece, and maybe more. It will take all my pin money for a month. No more soda water for a while, unless some one treats me."

"I suppose we ought to be thankful to get home at all," Dimple spoke up.

"Yes, when you consider it in that light, we're let off cheaply enough," Callie replied. "Oh, dear, where is that spring?"

"Just beyond that turn," Emma told her. And they toiled on till they reached the spot where the cold water bubbled out from a pebbly hollow under an old tree.

"We must cool off before we drink," Libbie warned them. "We'll bathe our faces and hands, and sit here for a while. We are so overheated we ought not to drink right away."

"It's very hard not to," said Callie, "but I suppose you are right."

"I am as hungry as I am thirsty," Libbie remarked. "If we only had one biscuit apiece, it would be something."

They had refreshed themselves with the cool spring water, and were idly sitting under a tree, when Dimple sprang up, crying, "I see something!" And she scrambled up the bank to a ledge beyond. "Girls! girls! here are lots of huckleberries," she called.

"Are you sure?"

"Certain sure. I wish you'd see. Come up." And they clambered up to the spot to find that she spoke truly: there was a patch of huckleberry bushes full of fruit. They set to work with a will and bore their feast down to the spring, near which they seated themselves on a fallen log.

"Did you ever taste anything so good?" said Emma. "I never care much for huckleberries at home, but I shall never despise them again."

Being refreshed they took up their journey again. Weary and warm they at length reached home, glad indeed to see the familiar streets, shady and quiet.

"I am going to see you safely in your mother's hands," Callie assured Dimple; "for it was my fault that you got into trouble. I had no business to tempt you."

"But you only meant it out of kindness," replied Dimple, appreciatively. "I think you were very good to want us; and it would have been all right if the boat had not floated off that way."

"But we did float off, and I want to explain matters to your mother."

"I'll give you the dollar I have in my bank," said Dimple.

"No, wait till we find out about the other man; the one who

owns the boat. When he understands that we didn't mean any harm, and that it was an accident, perhaps he won't charge for the boat, and then we'll only have to pay eighty cents apiece. I don't want to take any money of yours if I can help it."

"Oh, but you must. I'm sure mamma will say so."

"Well, we'll see. Just look how nicely your frock has dried. It doesn't look bad at all. A little limp maybe, but it's better that than muddy. I hope your mamma isn't very much worried. I don't believe it is so late after all." And although it seemed to Dimple that she had been days away from home, she was surprised to find that it was only about four o'clock, when hot and hungry they arrived at home.

Callie made her excuses and apologies as contritely as possible, and Mrs. Dallas was so relieved to find that nothing worse had happened, that she said very little in the way of reproof to the two runaways.

"You must never go down to the river again, my children," she said; "that is, unless papa or I, or some trustworthy person is with you. I should have forbidden you to go this time, but you have never ventured there before."

"I know, mamma," replied Dimple, "but it was so easy getting there from Mr. Atkinson's place, that we were there before we knew it. Was it 'Didn't think,' mamma?"

"Not exactly. I suppose you hardly realized that you were doing wrong since there were older girls with you, and it was more of an accident than actual wrongdoing. I think we shall have to keep you at home hereafter, for it seems very easy for little folks to get into trouble when they are away from their mothers. You have your own garden and your own little house to play in, so I think we must set the bounds there, and only allow you to go outside our premises by special invitation."

"Not even to Mr. Atkinson's?"

Amy E. Blanchard

"No, I think not, dear. It is safer for you at home. Mamma has been greatly worried and distressed, and I am sure you do not want her to pass through such an anxious time again. It is for mamma's sake, dear, as well as your own, that she keeps you close to her. Suppose you had fallen overboard." She drew the child nearer to her, while her eyes grew moist at the thought.

"Dear, dear mamma, I'll never go away again without your leave. I don't want to make you unhappy, mamma. I do love you."

"I know you do, darling; but little girls sometimes forget that it is more by the doing than by the saying that their mothers are made aware of their love. You know papa always tells you that if you really love your parents, you will do the things that please them, otherwise, no matter how much you say 'I love you,' it doesn't mean anything."

Dimple looked very sober, and Florence, too, listened to all this with a very grave face. It had really been a very trying day for the two little cousins, and now that they were safe, they realized how uncomfortable it had been. Therefore, from that time there never was a question of their going outside the gate without permission, and Mr. Atkinson's place was no longer visited unless by his express invitation on Saturday afternoons.

"I feel as if I had been sort of ungrateful," said Dimple, the next day after their rescue. "I just love my home, Florence, and somehow I don't feel a bit bad about not going to Mr. Atkinson's. I believe I know exactly how the little birdies feel when they get back to the nest, after they have been trying to fly. I hope I shall never go so far away again, until I am much older." And the two returned contentedly to their old playground, only too glad to feel the security of familiar sights and sounds.

CHAPTER IX

DOWN TOWN

"Don't you want to go down town for me, girls?" said Mrs. Dallas, one pleasant morning. "I can't send Bubbles very well."

"Oh, yes," said Dimple. "What are we to get?"

"Several things," replied her mother. "Go and get ready and I will tell you."

"May we take Celestine and Rubina?" asked Florence.

"I don't think I would, for you will have packages, and they will be in the way."

"Don't let's take them anyhow, Florence," said Dimple. "I was thinking this morning that their frocks are too thick for summer." So they ran off to get ready.

"Now," said Mrs. Dallas, as they came back, "I want you to go to Fink's and get me four yards of trimming like this sample; if they haven't exactly like it, the nearest will do. Then I want you to get me four lemons. You may go to old Mrs. Wills for those, and if she has any fresh eggs you may get a dozen, and—oh, yes, a bottle of vanilla extract. Now don't be too long, for I shall want to use some of the things this morning."

They promised, and went off without delay. It was a pleasant

July morning, and they started gaily down the street, which was shaded by trees and bordered on each side by pretty cottages, with gardens in front.

"There is Mrs. Brown," said Dimple; "let's cross over, Florence, she will be sure to stop us if we don't."

"Who is Mrs. Brown?" asked Florence.

"Oh, she's a woman," returned Dimple. "I suppose she is very nice, but she is so solemn, and is always telling me that she hopes I will grow up to be a comfort to my mother and not a care and burden; and she always says it as if there wasn't the least doubt but that I would be a care and a burden, and I don't like her. Do you know mamma and Mrs. Hardy have been friends for over twenty years, and mamma is Rock's godmother?"

"How do you know?"

"Mamma told me. I asked her how she came to know Rock's mother, and she said she used to know her when she was a little girl like me—and when they were young ladies they were great friends. Then mamma was married and came here, and Rock's mother was married and went to California. When her husband died she came back to Baltimore to live. Here is Fink's; we have to go in here."

This was the largest dry goods shop in the town, and the clerks all knew Dimple.

"What can we do for you this morning, Miss Dallas?" said one of them, leaning over the counter.

"Mamma wants four yards of this trimming," said Dimple, holding out her sample.

The man took it, turned it over to examine both sides, and took down a box.

"Four yards, did you say?"

"Yes," said Dimple.

He measured it off, saying, "Don't you want some cards? We have some just in with a lot of goods."

"I would rather have a box," said Dimple; "for I have a new doll, and I want it to put her sashes in."

"You don't object to having both, do you?" said he. "Suppose I put the cards in the box. How would that do?"

"Oh, that would be very nice," said Dimple; "you are very kind."

As he went off, she turned to Florence and said in a low tone, "I didn't like to ask him for two boxes, but I will give you the cards."

"No matter," said Florence. "I don't care very much for a box."

However, when the man returned he had two boxes with four pretty cards in each.

"Thank you so much," said the girls, highly pleased.

"He is a real nice man," said Florence, when they were in the street. "I didn't believe he would think of me."

"Yes, I think he is nice," said Dimple; "besides he has known me ever since I was a baby; he mightn't be so nice to a stranger."

They next came to a little low brown building with one window. As they went in at the door, a small bell over it tinkled and a voice said, "In a minute."

While they waited they looked about the shop, which was

quite a curiosity to Florence. In the window were jars of candy, red and white, gingerbread horses, shoestrings, oranges, lemons, and dolls strung along in a line, the largest in the middle and the smallest at each end; besides these there were tops, whistles, writing paper, pencils, scrap pictures, and a variety of other things, all jumbled up together. Inside, the glass case and the shelves were full, and from the ceiling hung rolls of cotton in tissue paper, toy wagons, jumping-jacks and hoops.

"What a funny place," whispered Florence; but just then a funnier old woman came in. Her face looked like a withered apple, it was so wrinkled and rosy; her eyes were bright and her grey hair was combed back under a high white cap. As she came behind the counter, Florence saw that one of her hands was very much scarred, and the fingers bent. She wondered what had happened to it.

"Well, little Dallas girl, it's you, is it? And how is my pretty with her dimples and curls? Hm! Hm! Hm! The little Dallas girl," said the old woman.

"Mamma wants four lemons, Mrs. Wills," said Dimple.

"Four lemons; four—four—" said the old woman, going to a box and taking them out.

"And she wants to know if you have any fresh eggs?"

"Fresh eggs. Hm! Hm! Fresh eggs. How many? I'll see."

"A dozen if you have them."

"Well, we'll have to go and find them, little girls. Who is the other little girl?"

"My cousin," said Dimple.

"A Dallas?"

"No; her name is Florence Graham."

"Graham, Graham. A Dallas and a Graham. Come you two, then, and we'll see if we can find any eggs."

They followed Mrs. Wills through the back room into the yard. The room they passed through was very clean, and held a stove with a little tin kettle on it, a bed with a patchwork quilt, a shining little table and several chairs with flowers painted on them.

The yard was quite a curiosity, and seemed to be given up entirely to pigeons and chickens, who made a great fuss, flying up on the old woman's shoulder and pecking at her; while an old duck waddled solemnly after, giving a quack once in a while to let them know she was there.

Mrs. Wills took them to the hen-house, and told them where to look for eggs.

As Dimple had been there before, she knew where to look, and they soon made up the dozen.

The old duck followed them into the house, and was waddling after them into the shop, when Mrs. Wills with a "Shoo! Shoo!" drove her out.

"Now, Dallas girl, and Graham girl," said Mrs. Wills, "does the mother need anything else to-day?"

"There was something else," said Dimple, "but I can't think what. Can you, Florence?"

"There were four things, I know," said Florence. "But I don't remember the fourth."

"A—apples, B—brooms, C—crackers, D—dust-pans," went on Mrs. Wills, rapidly, and then paused.

"No; not any of those," said Dimple.

"E—extract," said Mrs. Wills.

"Yes, that's it. You have guessed, Mrs. Wills, vanilla, please."

"E—extract, E—extract," said the old woman, as she hunted in a dark corner.

"And C—cocoanut cakes. Red or white?" she asked, opening the case.

"White," said Dimple. "But Mrs. Wills—"

"Tut! Tut! Don't you say it; don't you say it, or I'll take back my eggs," she said, as she handed each of the children a cake.

"Thank you, Mrs. Wills. When I'm grown-up I'll make you a great big cake and send it to you," said Dimple.

That pleased the old woman mightily, and she nodded good-bye to them, saying, "Lemons, eggs and extract," over and over to herself.

"What a ridiculous old woman!" said Florence. "Is she crazy?"

"No," said Dimple. "But she is queer. She is good, though, and mamma always buys everything from her that she can, and she feels so bad if I don't take the things she offers me that I have to accept them."

"What is the matter with her hand?"

"She burned it trying to save her child from burning."

"Did she save it?"

"No; and that is what makes her so queer. She has never been the same since."

"My! how warm it is getting," said Florence. "I am glad we have broad brimmed hats. Let's hurry home. There is your Mrs. Brown again."

"Oh, dear!" said Dimple. "Let us turn up this street; it is just as near to go home this way." So they turned the corner and reached home before Mrs. Brown knew which way they had gone.

"Suppose we watch Sylvy make cake," said Dimple, when they had delivered their packages. "She always lets me watch her. And then we can scrape the bowl. Don't you like to?"

"I never do at home," said Florence. "Our cook is so cross and mamma does not like me to go into the kitchen."

"My mamma doesn't care; she lets me go whenever I please, and sometimes I help Bubbles clean knives and do such things, so she can get through, and play with me sooner."

"Sylvy, we are coming to watch you make cake; may we?"

"I'm not a carin'!" said Sylvy. "Git 'round on the other side of the table."

"See her break the eggs," said Florence. "Could you do it, Dimple? I'd be sure to get the yolks all mixed with the whites, and she just turns one half into the other as easily."

"I'd be afraid to try," said Dimple; "but when I am a little bigger, I mean to make a cake myself. I believe I could now if I had some one to tell me."

"I wouldn't try just yet," said Sylvy, briskly beating the whites of the eggs to a froth.

"Could you, Sylvy, when you were a little girl?" asked Florence.

"Laws, no. I was nigh as big as I am now, and then I made a poor fist at it," said Sylvy, laughing at the recollection.

"What was the matter?" asked Dimple.

"Too much butter and sugar, and not enough flour; it rose up beautiful at first and then down it went; when I took it out of the oven it was like taffy. I felt plum bad, I tell you; but I did better next time;" so saying, she turned her cake into the pans and giving each of the children a spoon, bade them take the bowl between them out on the steps, and "lick" to their hearts' content.

"You aren't going to make another cake right away, are you, Sylvy?" asked Dimple, looking up from her bowl. "And—oh, Florence, see all those turnovers. Are you really going to make another cake, Sylvy?"

"Yass, miss, some suveral of 'em."

"What for?"

"Yo' ma done tole me to," replied Sylvy, with a smile.

"I'm going to ask her about it. I know she doesn't intend we shall eat them all. Perhaps there is going to be a church supper, or a strawberry festival, or something. Come on, Florence, let's go and see about it." And throwing down their spoons, they went to hunt up Mrs. Dallas.

They found her in the dining-room, making salad dressing, and upon the table was a newly-boiled ham, and a quantity of chopped chicken.

"There, now, mamma is doing something about eating, too," exclaimed Dimple. "I'd just like to know what it is all for. Won't you tell us, mamma? Are you going to have a tea or anything like that?"

"Not exactly like that; but we are going on a picnic."

"Oh! oh! a picnic! Tell us, mamma. Who is going? Are we children to go?"

"Yes. You children, Mrs. Hardy and Rock, the Spears, the Neals, and the Jacksons. Mr. Atkinson, too, I think."

"Which Jacksons?"

"Mr. David Jackson's family. Mr. Atkinson is not sure of being here, but he hopes to be able to get off."

"Oh, good! Tell us some more, mamma."

"We are going to start early to-morrow afternoon, if it is pleasant. We will take supper with us. We are going up the river to the island, and have our meal there."

"Fine! fine! Oh, Florence, you have never been to the island, and it is just lovely there. I think you are very good to let us go, mamma, after our running away in a boat."

"Who ever heard of any one's running away in a boat?" laughed Mrs. Dallas. "Now be good children, and keep out of the way, for Sylvy and I have a lot to do."

"We'll be good as possible, mamma, but just one more question: are you going to take Bubbles?"

"I hadn't thought of it."

"Oh, do, please; she'd be a lot of help, and she'd simply jump out of her skin if she thought she would be allowed to go."

"Then we'd better let her stay in her skin. She would be very uncomfortable without it, even in this warm weather."

"Please, mamma."

Amy E. Blanchard

Mrs. Dallas considered for a moment, and then said: "Well, yes, upon the whole, I think it would be rather a good plan, but she must not neglect her work to-day. If she gets through all that she has to do by the time we start she may go, but not otherwise. She will have extra work to-day, because Sylvy is more than usually busy."

"May we help her a little bit? We could clean the knives, and shell the peas."

"I think that would be very kind if you did."

"And may we tell her?"

"If you like."

The two little girls ran off to where Bubbles was washing out dish towels by the kitchen door. "Bubbles! Bubbles! You are going on a picnic," cried Dimple.

Bubbles dropped the dish towel she was dousing up and down in the water. "Me, Miss Dimple? Me? Who say so?"

"Mamma. There is to be a picnic to-morrow, and you are to go along with us. Aren't you glad?"

"Hm! Hm! I reckon I is. All dem cakes an' pies an' good eatin's, an' I gwine have some fo' dey gits mashed up an' soft, an' I gwine wait on de ladies and gent'mans. Ain't dat fine?" She gave a twist to her towel and shook it out with a snap. Then she was overtaken by a sudden fear. "Yuh ain't a-foolin' me, is yuh?"

"No, of course not. I wouldn't be so mean as to fool you about such a thing. But mamma says you mustn't dawdle to-day. So hurry up and get those towels done. Sylvy is going to be awfully busy, so you'll have to help her, but we're going to clean the knives for you, and shell the peas. Bring them down to the little house; we're going down there. We might set the table, too, Florence."

"Thanky, ma'am, Miss Dimple. Thanky, Miss Flo'ence." Bubbles' face was beaming, and her slim, black legs went scudding into the house with more than their usual agility.

"I shouldn't wonder if Rock were to come over, Florence," said Dimple; "then he can help us to shell the peas, so we can have some time to play. Rock will want to talk over the picnic, and he will want to see how the garden is coming on. I think the pumpkin vine is coming up. I can't tell whether it is that or a weed, but Rock will know."

"Rock always thinks of such nice plays; I hope he will come," returned Florence; and, indeed, they had hardly established themselves on the porch of the little house before the boy's cheery whistle was heard, and the three children, after faithfully fulfilling the promise to Bubbles to relieve her of some of her tasks, determined to invent a new play.

"I'll tell you what we'll do," said Rock. "We'll dig a cave over here, and we'll pretend a company of bandits live in it, and they will capture one of your dolls. Then we will go to the rescue."

"Who'll be the bandits?"

"Why, let me see. We'll take sticks of wood; little branches with two prongs, like this; they make the legs, you see; and then we'll stick on something round for the heads, turnips or onions or something like that."

"There aren't any turnips this time of year," returned Dimple, "and onions smell so strong. We can get potatoes, though, and they have eyes, so I should think they would make very good heads."

Rock laughed. "So they will."

"I'll go and see if mamma will let me have—how many?"

"Oh, half a dozen or so."

Dimple started for the house; then suddenly remembered that she had promised not to bother her mother, and she stood still for a moment. But the idea of the bandits was too alluring, and so she proceeded to the house, putting her head timidly in at the dining-room door, where her mother was still busy.

"Mamma," she said, "are potatoes very expensive?"

"No, not very. What a funny question. Did you come all the way in here to ask that?"

"No, mamma, not exactly; but do they cost too much for you to give us half a dozen for our bandits?"

"For your bandits! What do you mean?"

"Why, we are going to have a lovely play—Rock made it up— and we can't have any bandits unless we have heads for them, and I said potatoes would do, because they have eyes. May we have half a dozen?"

Mrs. Dallas smiled. "Yes, but you must not ask Sylvy or Bubbles to get them for you."

"I'll get them if you will tell me where they are."

"They are down in the cellar. Please, Dimple, don't bother me again. Try to play without coming up after things all the time."

"Yes, mamma," Dimple replied, very meekly. "I wouldn't have come this time if it had been for anything but the bandits."

Mrs. Dallas let her go, and then called her back, for she had seen a little wistful look in the child's face when her mother spoke shortly. "Come, kiss me, dear," she said. "I want you to know that you are quite welcome to the potatoes. They will make very inexpensive and harmless playthings, and I hope your bandits will turn out just as you want them to."

Dimple gave her a grateful hug.

"You may stop in the kitchen and get a turnover apiece for you three children. Tell Sylvy I said you might."

"Oh, mamma, how dear you are," and the happy little face disappeared.

The six potato-headed bandits proved most venturesome creatures, and kept their captive safe from her would-be rescuers, till she was redeemed by the payment of a hundred pieces of gold, represented by buttercup petals, and the morning passed so quickly that the children could scarcely believe it, when Bubbles came—as they had told her to do—to tell them it was time to set the dinner-table.

"Shall I fill up the cave?" Rock asked.

"Oh no, we might want to use it again," Dimple decided. "That was such a lovely, exciting play, Rock."

"Then we'd better cover up the cave. Some one might step in it, and get hurt."

After hunting around, an old battered tin pan was found, which was laid over the entrance, but, alas! it was not proof against Bubbles' unfairy-like tread, for she stepped on it that very evening, and down she went, but, as luck had it, she did nothing worse than scratch her toes upon the very rough body of the bandit chief; although, be it confessed, he fared worse by the encounter than she did, for he had both legs broken beyond hope of saving. The next morning he was carefully carried away to a hospital and devotedly nursed by one of Dimple's dolls; but he never recovered, though he lingered for several days. His funeral was quite a magnificent affair, and he was buried with proper ceremonies under the very tree upon which he originally grew.

CHAPTER X

THE PICNIC

The children awoke on the morning of the day set for the picnic, to view, with anxious eyes, a grey sky.

"Oh, if it should rain, wouldn't it be just too bad for anything," said Florence. "I should be so dreadfully disappointed, shouldn't you, Dimple?"

"Yes, I am afraid so," returned Dimple, despondently, watching the smoke rising from a distant chimney. Then more cheerfully, "See Florence, I don't believe it will rain, for that smoke is going straight up. You know that is a sign it is going to clear. Maybe it is only misty and not cloudy."

This it proved to be, for, as the day advanced, the sun came out and it was as beautiful an afternoon as one could wish to see. Therefore very gaily they started forth to meet the rest of the party down at the river's brink.

"Oh, there's Mr. Atkinson," cried Dimple, catching sight of this gentleman's pleasant face, "I am so glad he could come. I wonder if he sees us. I hope we can go in his boat, don't you, Florence?"

"Yes, indeed, I do. He sees us. He is waving his hat."

The two little girls ran forward and to their satisfaction were

Amy E. Blanchard

helped into Mr. Atkinson's boat with Mr. and Mrs. Dallas and Bubbles as fellow-passengers, Bubbles grinning from ear to ear and looking very spick and span in a clean pink calico frock and a white apron. A string of blue beads adorned her neck; she had added it as a finishing touch to her toilet.

The boats pushed off and, after an hour's rowing, the party of picnickers landed at a pretty little island in the river. It was covered with trees and underbrush, but not so densely as to prevent their finding a space big enough for a camping ground where they could build a fire and spread their supper.

Most of the party preferred to go out on the river to fish, for some fine black bass could be caught here. Dimple, however, preferred to stay behind with Mrs. Dallas and one or two of the other ladies, even though Mr. Atkinson said he would bait her hook for her, and would lend her his finest line and reel.

"I feel so sorry for the poor little earth worms, first, and for the fish afterward, that I don't believe I should enjoy it," Dimple said, seriously.

"But you can eat a piece of bass after it is cooked, can't you?" Mr. Atkinson returned, smiling.

"Yes, if I don't see him caught."

"Your little girl reminds me of those very tender-hearted children, who, when they saw the picture of the Christian martyrs, were overcome with pity, not for the martyrs, no indeed, but because there was one poor dear lion that hadn't any martyr to eat," Mr. Atkinson said to Mr. Dallas.

"That was a little extreme, I admit," returned Mr. Dallas, laughing, "but we do try to cultivate a humane spirit in our little daughter, and you may be sure she will never wear a stuffed bird in her hat when she grows older."

Mr. Atkinson nodded in approval. "I'm glad of that," he

returned, "and I must say I think useless sport is wicked, but when one wants fish for food, I think he may be excused the catching. And so, Dimple, it resolves itself into your going without the fish or the fishing, does it?"

Dimple nodded. She didn't exactly understand, but she supposed he meant that if she wanted the fish for supper, she'd better remain where she could not see them caught.

Florence, however, had less compunction, and consented to go out in the boat, though she wasn't sure whether or not she should want to catch any fish. But Rock, like most boys, was very eager for the sport, and hoped he would be able to catch the first fish, and also wanted it to be the biggest caught.

"May Bubbles and I go anywhere on the island that we want?" Dimple asked her mother, after they had watched the boats start off.

Mrs. Dallas, with Mrs. Hardy's help, was putting up a hammock between two of the big trees. "I think it will be perfectly safe," she replied, after a moment's thought. "The island isn't very big, and you will not go too near the water's edge, will you? I can see you from here—I suppose in whatever direction you go."

"I will keep away from the water, mamma, although I should dearly like to paddle about."

"You can take off your shoes and stockings and paddle right here on this bit of shore when you come back from your exploring trip. I can watch you then, and shall feel perfectly easy about you."

"Where are the lunch baskets, mamma?"

"Over there behind that tree."

"What is that covered up with that grey blanket?"

Amy E. Blanchard

"Something Mr. Atkinson brought."

"I didn't see it in our boat. May I peep at it?"

"No, dear, I think I wouldn't. It isn't just the thing to indulge one's curiosity about such matters. Mr. Atkinson had it sent up here, and as he meant it as a sort of a little secret for you children, it wouldn't be polite to try to find it out."

So Dimple with her little maid, walked away, not, however, without several backward looks at the grey blanket.

There was not very much to see on the island, after all, for it was a small place, and the most interesting discovery they made was a pile of big rocks at the upper end of the narrow strip of land. Here they established themselves to watch the boats and the fishers.

"I think Rock has caught a fish," exclaimed Dimple, when she had been watching for some time. "See, Bubbles, he is hauling in his line as fast as he can. There goes the reel again. Oh, I hope if he must catch them, that he will catch big ones. See that lovely red flower growing down there between the rocks. I wish you would get it for me, Bubbles, and then we will go back to where mamma is. I am as hungry as I don't know what, and I want to ask mamma for a turnover or a biscuit or something. Get me the flower, Bubbles, and I'll watch to see if Rock really did catch a fish."

Bubbles promptly obeyed, but she had just stooped to pick the flower when she heard a piercing shriek from Dimple. Mrs. Dallas heard it, too, and came running in the greatest alarm, to find, when she reached the spot, Dimple almost paralyzed with fright, continuing her screams, while Bubbles, dancing about, getting more and more excited every minute, was valiantly hurling pieces of rock at a large black snake.

"Hyar come anudder," she cried, as a stone went flying through the air. "Take dat. Hit yuh, didn't it? Skeer Miss

Dimple outen her senses, will yuh? Yuh gre't, ugly black crittur!" and rock after rock came with such force and precision that the unfortunate snake, in a few minutes, was "daid as a do' nail," as Bubbles expressed it.

Dimple clung to her mother, trembling with fright, even after the snake was killed.

"Is it dead, really dead? Oh, Bubbles!" she quavered. "What would I have done if you hadn't been so brave?"

Bubbles laughed. "Dat wan't no snake to pison yuh," she said. "It couldn't hurt yuh. All it could do was to race yuh."

"Don't talk about it," said Dimple, shuddering. "Do let us leave it, and go back."

But Bubbles was too proud of her performance to allow it to be set aside; so she picked up the snake, and started to carry it back on a forked stick.

On the way, however, she too fell into a fright at sight of an innocent little land terrapin traveling along with his house on his back. "Don't tech it, don't, Miss Dimple," she cried in terror. "Dey has de evilest eyes. I wouldn't tech one fer nothin'."

"But you aren't afraid of snakes," replied Dimple, "and these little terrapins are much more harmless." Nevertheless Bubbles had in some way acquired a superstition about "Bre'r Tarrapin," from Sylvy, who, like most colored people, stood in terror of the innocent creatures.

But when the boats returned, the big snake, hanging over the limb of a tree, was triumphantly displayed and attested to Bubbles' courage; so that she was made very proud by the praise she received for having killed it, Dimple generously refraining from saying anything about the terrapin.

Amy E. Blanchard

Although Rock did not catch the first fish, he caught the biggest one, and was quite proud of it.

There was a fire built, and the fish, nicely cleaned, were cooked over the coals. Florence thought all this delightful. She had never enjoyed such an experience, and watched the proceedings with the greatest pleasure. Every one was ready to enjoy the supper when it was prepared, saying that fish never tasted so good, and that the coffee, made in a very ordinary tin coffee-pot, could not be improved.

Dimple whispered to Florence that there was a secret under the grey blanket; and that she half suspected what it was, but she didn't intend to look. Even a delighted giggle from Bubbles did not cause her to turn her head, but when that small hand-maiden, who was bustling about waiting on every one, offered her a saucer of ice cream, Dimple exclaimed, "I guessed it! I guessed it to myself."

"Guessed what?" said Mr. Atkinson, at her side.

"Guessed that it was an ice cream freezer under the blanket," returned Dimple.

"Oho! so you've been trying to find out, have you?"

"No. I didn't try. I only hoped," replied Dimple, gravely. At which Mr. Atkinson laughed heartily; just why, Dimple was puzzled to discover.

When the supper was over and the baskets repacked, they played all manner of games till the great round moon rose over the river, and then they rowed home, singing as they floated along in the silvery moonlight.

Florence and Dimple sat side by side, in a sort of waking dream; and Bubbles dreamed too, as was very evident when the boat landed, for she was sound asleep, and had to be called and shaken before she knew where she was. Then she blundered along behind the others, still so sleepy that she forgot to take off her precious blue beads when she went to bed, and in the night the string broke; consequently when she awoke in the morning she found the beads straggling over the floor and strewing the sheets.

"Didn't we have a good time?" said Florence, looking out on the moonlight, as she stood at the window in Dimple's room.

"Yes," was Dimple's reply, "all but the snake. I don't like snakes."

But the next evening it was evident that Bubbles still bore the subject of snakes in her mind. Mr. and Mrs. Dallas had gone out. Dimple, Florence and Bubbles were sitting on the floor by one of the front windows.

The air was full of the scent of the honeysuckle, and the katydids were contradicting each other in the trees.

"What quarrelsome things they are," said Florence. "Do you suppose they will ever find out whether katy did or not? I'd like to know what she did, anyhow."

"Or what she didn't," said Dimple. "Bubbles, are you asleep?" giving her a shake.

"Thinkin'," said Bubbles, sitting up straight and rubbing her eyes.

"Then what are you rubbing your eyes for?"

"Cause it's dark. I can't see good," returned Bubbles.

"I declare," Dimple said, "I never know what to do with myself when mamma goes out; it seems to me she is very intimate with Mrs. Hardy. Florence, suppose you tell a story."

"Oh, I can't," replied Florence. "I never could. I never know

Amy E. Blanchard

what to tell about. You tell."

"I don't know any except Cinderella and the Seven Swans, and those. Bubbles will have to do it. Go on Bubbles, you've got to tell us a story."

"Laws! Miss Dimple," giggled Bubbles.

"You needn't 'laws,' you know you can, for you've often told them to me; now begin, right away; it will keep you awake if it doesn't do anything else."

"Well," said Bubbles, smoothing down her apron, "oncet they was a bummelybee, and a snake, and a bird."

"What kind of a bird?" interrupted Florence.

"Erra—erra—bluebird," said Bubbles.

"All right, go on."

"The snake wanted fur to git the bluebird, and the bummely-bee was a-flyin, and a-buzzin' so, it made such a 'straction the snake couldn't git fixed fur to chawm the bird nohow.

"Jess yuh quit yo' foolin'," said the snake.

"I no foolin', " said the bummelybee, 'what's got yuh anyhow?'

"I ain't had no brekfuss," said the snake.

"Well go 'long 'n git it; I'm not a hinderin'."

"Yes, yuh is," said the snake, "I can't do nothin' fur yo' buzzin'."

"Then the bummelybee flown off, but he didn't go very fur, he wanted to see what the snake was up to. He kinder suspicioned it wasn't up to no good, so he jess watched the snake, and bimeby he seen the bluebird come up as peart as anythin', and he set down on the limb of a tree."

Here Bubbles stopped to take breath, and then went on,

"Well, he seen the snake a-crawlin' along the grass, a-crawlin', a-crawlin', as crafty till it got right in front of the bluebird, and the bluebird he jess set and looked, and didn't move, or say nothin'.

"'Hm! hm!' says Mr. Bummelybee, 'hit's time I was a movin'," so he made fur the snake and giv' him one sting on the haid, and he jess rolled up he eyes, and quirled up ontil the grass; and the bluebird said, "I'm much debliged of you, Mr. Bummelybee. I'm glad to perform yo' acquaintance. I was jess about as nigh chawmed as a bird could be."

"'Don't say no more about it,' said Mr. Bummelybee, and off he flown."

"I didn't know bumblebees could sting," said Florence.

"Law now don't they?" said Bubbles, "mebbe they doesn't, hit might a been a wass, wasses sting I know. Come to think of it, hit was a wass."

"Is that all of it?" asked Dimple. "I don't think it is a very long story."

"Laws, Miss Dimple, you didn't reckon that was all," said Bubbles, loftily. "I laid out to tell more, soon ez my tongue got rested."

"Rest it then, and go on," said Dimple, settling back against a chair, with her hands behind her head.

"Well," said Bubbles, going on with her story, "the wass he flown off, and the bluebird he flown off, and after a while the bluebird he met a squirl. 'Howdy?' says he. 'Howdy,' says the squirl. 'How's all to yo' house?'

"Tollable, thank you," says the bluebird. 'Ef yuh see a wass come along—' Laws, Miss Dimple, I can't get along without'n hit's being a bummely," said she, stopping short.

"Well, have it a bummely then," said Dimple. "You don't care, do you, Florence?"

"No," said Florence, "have it a bummely if you want to, Bubbles."

"Well," says the bluebird, 'ef you see a bummelybee, don't you let nobody take his honey from him, fur he's a pertickeler fren' of mine.' He was sorter shamed to let on to the squirl how nigh chawmed he was.

"I promise, cross my heart," says the squirl, and Mr. Bluebird flown off.

"Aftern awhile, up flown Mr. Bummely, and smack behind him comes a little boy layin' out to git his honey.

"Mr. Bummely he flown along and went to hide hissef in a big flower. That's jess what the boy wanted. 'Now I've got yuh,' says he, but he was too forward, fur the squirl clim' down the tree and popped onto the boy's haid jess ez he was gwine to take off his hat to ketch Mr. Bummely, and Mr. Bummely he flown off, and Mr. Squirl he laugh, and Mr. Boy he got mad, and made tracks fur home, and that's all."

The girls laughed, and hearing Sylvy call her, Bubbles went out.

"Isn't she funny?" said Florence. "I never could have made up a story like that, could you, Dimple?"

"No," said Dimple, "she tells me the funniest ones sometimes, so mixed up, and I laugh till I can scarcely speak, and she sings the most absurd songs; she gets the words all twisted, she has no idea what they mean. Oh! Florence, I do believe there is a bat in the hall. I hope to goodness it won't come in here."

Florence screamed and hid her head under the piano, while Dimple took refuge in the same place, and called loudly for Bubbles, who came running in with Sylvy after her.

"What's de matter? Where are yuh?" they cried.

"Oh, a bat! a bat!" shrieked Florence, as the creature came swooping in from the hall, beating its wings against the wall.

Sylvy, armed with a broom, and Bubbles, with a duster, soon put an end to the poor bat, and the girls came out from their hiding-place.

"I suppose it is silly to be afraid of them, but they nearly frighten me to death," said Dimple.

"So they do me," Florence said, "and spiders too. Ugh! it makes cold chills run down my back to think of one; let's go to bed, Dimple. We can undress anyhow, and sit in our night-gowns and talk, if we want to."

This Dimple agreed to, and they went upstairs to their rooms to find on the bureau two little white paper packages addressed to "Miss Florence Graham," and "Miss Eleanor Dallas."

"Papa did it," said Dimple, "it is just like him; let's see what is inside. No, we'll guess. I say chocolates."

"I say burnt almonds: no, marshmallows," said Florence, giving her package a little squeeze. "Marshmallows and chocolates," exclaimed Florence, as she untied the little pink string and peeped in.

"So are mine," said Dimple. "I don't think we had better eat them all to-night, do you? Suppose we count them and take out some for to-morrow. One, two, three, twelve chocolates, and sixteen marshmallows. How many have you?"

"Thirteen chocolates and fifteen marshmallows," announced Florence.

"Well, let's eat six of them, and put the rest away."

So they were carefully counted out, and the packages retied.

"Now we will undress and sit here in our nightgowns, till we've eaten our candy," said Florence.

"Dear me," said Dimple, as the last one disappeared, "I wish we had said seven of them."

"Suppose we do say seven."

"Well, suppose we do," and the packages were again untied and again put up. They had hardly finished when Mrs. Dallas came in with a telegram in her hand.

"Not in bed yet?" said she.

"No, mamma, we have been eating candy. Did you see papa put it on the bureau?" said Dimple.

"Yes, and I have a piece of news for you. Your Uncle Heath will be here to-morrow."

"Uncle Heath! I am so glad. Is the telegram from him?"

"Yes, it just came, and he will be here to breakfast."

"How long will he stop?"

"Not very long. Now jump into bed and be ready to get up before he reaches here."

"Is your Uncle Heath your papa's brother?" asked Florence, when they were in bed.

"Yes. Oh! Florence, he is so nice."

"Is he young or old?"

"Not so very old, about forty, I think; he is two years older than papa, but he looks older; he has grey hair, a little bit grey, not very, and he looks like papa, only he has blue eyes.

"I wonder why he is coming," mused Dimple. "Now I think of it. I heard papa say yesterday, 'I am so glad for dear old Heath.' I wonder why. Don't grown folks know lots of things, Florence? And we have to just guess and wonder till they choose to tell us.

"Never mind, I am going to sleep, and I shall ask him myself to-morrow. Just think, Florence, he is in the cars now, and they are steaming along, coming nearer and nearer, while we lie still here and sleep. Good-night," and she turned over and was soon fast asleep.

CHAPTER XI

AN UNCLE AND A WEDDING

Dimple was up betimes the next morning. Creeping quietly out of bed, she left Florence sound asleep.

"Mamma," she whispered, softly, as she opened her mamma's door, "what time is it? Has Uncle Heath come?"

"It is half-past six," said her mamma, "and Uncle Heath will be here in half an hour."

"May I put on my blue frock?"

"Yes."

Dimple slipped back, and was not long in dressing. Florence sleepily opened her eyes as Dimple was ready to leave the room.

"Oh Dimple, are you dressed?" she said, sitting up in bed. "Has the bell rung?"

"No," said Dimple, "but Uncle Heath is coming, you know, and I want to meet him. Come down when you are ready."

Florence being wide awake by this time, concluded to get up, and Dimple ran downstairs, patting the baluster with one hand as she went.

When she reached the lowest step she was caught up by a pair of arms, and found her face close to her Uncle Heath's whiskers.

"Oh! Uncle Heath," she cried, "do let me hug you. I am so glad to see you. I'm gladder than anybody."

"I hope not," said her father from the doorway.

"Yes, I am," said Dimple, as her uncle carried her into the parlor, and held her on his knee. "Uncle Heath, are you very happy?"

"Indeed, I am," said he, laughing, as did Dimple's papa and mamma.

"Quite a home thrust," said her papa.

"The reason I asked," she went on, playing with her uncle's watch chain, "is, that I heard papa say the other day, 'I am so glad for dear old Heath.'"

"He has reason to be," responded her uncle. "Dimple, how should you like a new aunt and cousin?"

"Oh, uncle! Is it Rock?"

"Well, not Rock altogether," laughed he. "Rock's mother, as well."

"Please tell me, Uncle Heath."

"So I will, little girl. Rock's mother is going to be your grey-headed uncle's wife. That makes Rock your cousin, doesn't it?"

"Yes," said Dimple, cuddling up to him, "but you are not grey-headed, Uncle Heath, only grey-templed," she said, softly patting each side of his face.

"She seems perfectly satisfied," said he, looking at his brother.

"Perfectly," he answered. "You could not have pleased her better."

"But, Uncle Heath," said Dimple, "I didn't know you knew Mrs. Hardy."

"I knew her long ago, when she wasn't Mrs. Hardy, but Dora West. Long ago," he repeated, gently stroking her hair.

"Why didn't you marry her then?"

"I wanted to," said he, simply, "but I couldn't. Do you want to be bridesmaid, Dimple?"

"Oh, uncle! Could I?"

"Yes, indeed; and Rock groomsman. We are such a young, frivolous couple, we couldn't think of having a grown-up young lady for bridesmaid."

Dimple laughed, and sat in supreme content on her uncle's knee till the breakfast bell rang.

"Florence, I know all about it," she cried, as Florence came in, "and I am going to be bridesmaid, and I know why Uncle Heath is happy, and why Rock can be my cousin. Isn't it lovely?"

Florence looked puzzled, but after a clearer explanation agreed with Dimple that it was "perfectly lovely."

Rock came over after breakfast, with a message for Mrs. Dallas, and Dimple ran out to meet him, crying, "Oh, Rock! your papa is here, and you are going to be my cousin, really and truly. Did you know it?"

"Yes, I knew," said he, "and I'm real glad. Where is Mr. Dallas?"

"My Uncle Heath, or papa?"

"Your Uncle Heath."

"He has gone to see your mamma, I think. And oh, Rock! we are going to be bridesmaids, you and I. No, I mean I am going to be bridesmaid, and you groomsman."

"Yes, and something else I know, too," said Rock. "While mamma goes on her wedding trip I am to come here to stay."

"Oh! Rock," exclaimed Dimple, clapping her hands, "that will be lovely, too. How long?"

"Three days, I think."

"Won't we have good times?" laughed Dimple, dancing up and down. "Do come sit down and talk about it. Are you glad you are going to have my Uncle Heath for your papa?"

"Yes, indeed," said Rock.

"And are you going to live here?"

"No, in Baltimore."

"Oh, dear, that is all that spoils it."

"Never mind," said Rock. "I shouldn't wonder if we were to come here summers, and I'll tell you, Dimple, maybe your mother will let you come visit us next winter, and I will take you sleighing."

That comforted Dimple somewhat.

"Where is the wedding to be? I never thought to ask," said she.

"At church, at half-past nine Thursday morning. Then we come back to your house to breakfast, and mamma and Mr.

Dallas go away on the twelve o'clock train."

"When you say Mr. Dallas I think you mean my papa," said Dimple. "I wish you would call Uncle Heath papa."

"But he isn't my papa yet."

"Well, three days doesn't make much difference, and you need only say it to me."

"Well! papa and mamma," said Rock, laughing, "will be back Sunday evening, and Monday we all go away."

"Don't talk about that part of it. I don't want to think of it."

Here Dimple's mamma called her, and she went upstairs. "Wait till I come back, Rock," she said, as she went out, "I want to talk some more."

"What do you want with me, mamma?" she asked as she entered her mamma's room.

"I want to try on your bridesmaid frock."

"Oh, mamma! Is that it?" she exclaimed, as her mamma lifted a soft white mull from the bed.

"Yes, and you are to wear a white hat and carry a basket of flowers. Isn't it odd that my little daughter should be bridesmaid for some one who was once her mamma's bridesmaid, and who used to play with her when she was a little girl?"

Dimple laughed at the idea, as she put her arms through the arm-holes, and said, "It is all so funny, mamma, that I can't straighten it out at all. It is like a fairy tale, and, O! mamma, I look like a fairy in this frock. Isn't it lovely? I wish I might go down and show it to Rock and Florence."

"Very well, you may, only be very careful not to catch it on anything."

"I will be, mamma," and she danced off to display her finery.

"See, Rock! See, Florence! Don't I look almost like a fairy?" she exclaimed, as she went into the library, where they both were sitting, each in a big chair.

"Oh! you do look sweet!" they said, and Dimple smiled and blushed at the praise, quite delighted with herself; but presently she looked at Florence a little gravely, and said:

"Florence, I feel so selfish. Do you care very much that I am to be a bridesmaid, and you not?"

"No, indeed, for I am to be bridesmaid when my sister is married, anyhow, and I would so much rather see it all than to be right in it."

So Dimple went up to take off her frock quite reassured.

"Mamma, what are you going to wear? White, too?" she asked.

"No, grey, with pink roses; and Mrs. Hardy will wear pale lavender and white roses."

"I thought brides always wore white."

"Not always," answered her mamma.

Long before half-past nine on the eventful morning Dimple stood ready, slippers, hat and all; her basket of flowers tied with white ribbons on the piano; and she felt very grand, indeed, when the carriage, with Rock in it, drove around for her. She had been up by daybreak, around to the church with flowers, upstairs to see that her bridesmaid toilet was all right, down into the kitchen to ask Sylvy for a peep at the wedding cake, which, black with fruit inside and white with frosting out, stood on the sideboard.

Then there was the table to see, and little helpful things to do for her mamma, while she arranged it; flowers to gather, a great bowl of fresh roses in the centre.

Then it was such a delight, after she and Florence were dressed, to watch her mamma get ready; to see her dainty laces, and hold her flowers ready for her to pin on.

At last the great moment really arrived, and she found herself stepping up the aisle with Rock, feeling a little embarrassment, though it was a very quiet wedding, only a few near friends being present; but she bore herself very bravely, holding her flower basket very tightly, and keeping time with her slippered feet to the wedding march.

She did not dare even to look at Rock, but kept her eyes steadfastly cast down.

She and Rock were the first to get back to the house, and when the new Mrs. Dallas reached there, Dimple rushed up to her and gave her a frantic hug, calling her "dear Aunt Dora;" then as frantic a hug was bestowed upon her uncle.

She danced through the rooms like a will-o'-the-wisp, hardly willing to sit at the table long enough to eat anything at all.

When the bridal pair drove away to the depot, a shower of rice and old shoes were flung after them by all the children, Bubbles included.

After the house was quiet again, Dimple, Florence and Rock sat talking it all over in the parlor.

"Were you frightened when you walked up the aisle?" asked Florence.

"A little; but I thought about looking at my slippers, and

didn't see the people. Did I look all right?"

"Yes; as lovely as possible, and I never should have thought you were frightened. What did you do with the flowers? And, oh Dimple, who had the lovely little figure on top of the cake?"

"I know," said Rock. "I heard mamma tell Dimple's mother that the bridesmaid ought to have that; and I think so, too."

"Oh!" said Dimple. "I think you ought to have it, Rock."

"No, indeed. That would be a fine way to do, I must say. It is to be yours. Mamma said so, and that settles it."

"Well," said Dimple. "But I have so much, it seems to me. Florence, isn't it funny for Rock to have a new papa? Everything turns out so oddly. Don't you know how provoked we were that day when Bubbles told us that mamma was bringing a boy out to see us?"

"And now that boy is your cousin," said Rock.

"Yes; and I am glad, too," replied Dimple, giving his hand a little affectionate pat. "I never knew boys could be so nice, till I saw you."

Rock laughed. "That's a pretty big compliment," he said.

"It isn't a compliment; it's the truth."

"And a compliment can't be the truth, I suppose?"

"Why, I don't know. Can it?"

"Of course; though just flattering words aren't always the truth. I've heard ladies who came to see mamma say, 'What a sweet child your little one is!'" Rock said this very affectedly, and the girls laughed. "And you know," Rock went on, "they didn't know a thing about me; they just said it to make mamma feel pleased, and that's what I call flattery."

"Oh, yes; I think I see," said Dimple.

The three days that followed were very merry ones for the children. They frolicked from morning till night, and did more wonderful things than ever they had dreamed of doing before.

Rock was the nicest sort of comrade, and they got along without any fusses whatever. Sunday was their last day together, for Florence was to go the next day, too, under the care of Mr. and Mrs. Heath Dallas, and her trunk was standing, packed, ready to be sent.

"Won't we have a pew full this morning?" said Dimple, at the breakfast table. "Five people. Rock, you must sit between Florence and me. I can sit next to mamma, and Florence next to papa."

"Oh, no; let me sit by auntie," said Florence.

"Very well," said Dimple. "I can sit by papa just as well, and if I get sleepy I can tumble over on him."

Papa laughed and said it was a pleasant prospect for him.

The church windows were open, a soft breeze fluttered the leaves outside and the slow rustle of fans fluttered bonnet strings inside.

Dimple leaned her head back against the pew, and looked out at the white clouds drifting across the sky, so dreamily and softly; she heard the birds singing in the trees, and now and then came back to a consciousness of the minister's voice, and she caught a sentence here and there; but she could not fix her attention on the sermon at all; she was thinking of the dreaded to-morrow that would take her playmates away from her. The quiet and solemnity of the place only added to the sadness of her thoughts, and as the last hymn was being sung, the tears gathered in her eyes and dropped silently down on her book.

Finally she could stand it no longer, but slipped down on her knees, buried her face in the cushions, and fairly sobbed.

No one knew what was the matter, and Mrs. Dallas looked distressed, fearing she was ill. Mr. Dallas leaned down toward her, and whispered, "Are you ill, Dimple?"

But she shook her head, and when the hymn was ended, he drew her close to him, and put his arm around her, while she kept her face hidden on his shoulder.

No one could tell what ailed her, as every question only brought a fresh burst of tears, and she walked home in silence.

It was not until they were in the house, that she could tell what affected her.

Then her mother took her on her lap, and she had her cry out there, while Florence and Rock, looking much concerned, stood by.

"Tell me, daughter, what ails you," her mother said, pushing back the curls from the little tear-stained face.

"It was so solemn—and—I was thinking about everybody's going away to-morrow," she said, between her sobs. "Then they sang—'Where friend holds fellowship with friend. Though sundered far'—and all that—and I couldn't stand it any longer," and the tears still rained down her face.

At this Florence's eyes filled up, and she put her arms around Dimple, and they cried together, while it took Mrs. Dallas, Rock, and Mr. Dallas, all three, to comfort them.

"You will soon be going to school, Dimple," said her papa, "and then you will have ever so many playmates."

Amy E. Blanchard

"And you are coming to see us next winter," said Rock.

"And you will have mamma left, anyhow," said her mother, hugging her up close.

So among them all, the tears were dried; and before dinner was over, they were all laughing as joyously as ever.

The only excitement left was to watch for the arrival of Rock's papa and mamma, who were to come that evening.

In the meantime, while Rock and Florence were reading, Dimple heard Bubbles her Sunday lesson. She always taught her one of the hymns she had herself learned, and a Bible verse or two.

Bubbles was not very quick at learning the verses, but delighted in the hymns, and sang them with Dimple, with great vigor.

This afternoon, however, it was quite wearisome to Dimple, for her cry had given her a headache, and she cut the lesson very short so as to get back to Rock and Florence.

"I shouldn't like to be a teacher," she said, throwing herself down on the lounge.

"I should," said Florence. "I love my teacher at school dearly; she is the sweetest, dearest thing, we girls almost fight over her."

"Do you? How funny," said Dimple.

"Why, yes, we take her flowers, and candy, and big apples and oranges; sometimes her desk is full."

"I am afraid I shan't like my teacher," said Dimple.

"Do you know her?"

"Yes, a little; she has been here to tea. She isn't so awful, and I should like her, perhaps, if I didn't know I had to go to school to her."

"Do you know many of the girls?"

"One or two. You saw that girl who sat in front of us at church, she is one."

"You will get used to it real soon," said Rock. "I felt just as you do before I went to school, and it is worse for a boy; the other boys just go for him, and I had a hard time for the first few weeks, but now I like it first-rate."

"It is the getting used to it, that I dread," sighed Dimple; "that has to come first."

"No," said Rock, "papa and mamma come first, and it is nearly time for them now; let's go on the front porch and watch."

"It is so sunny there," said Dimple.

"Not if we sit at the end. Come on."

So they went out and took up positions at the end of the porch.

"I want to see mamma and Gertrude, and all, awfully," said Florence, "but, indeed I hate to leave here," looking around. "I shall miss the trees, and flowers, and all the sweet things."

"So shall I," said Rock. "What a good time we have had this summer."

"Yes. Haven't we?" said Dimple, looking sober.

"Don't talk about it any more," said Rock. "It makes my Cousin Eleanor feel bad."

This made Dimple smile, and presently they saw coming up the street a carriage, which they felt sure would stop.

They all ran down to the gate, and the carriage did draw up by the sidewalk, and Rock was the first to open the door of it, and in another minute was in his mother's arms.

Then they all went into the house, and made ready for tea.

All that evening Dimple sat with one arm around Florence; and, although Rock was so glad to see his mother, he said that he would have Dimple so short a time that he must sit by her, and the three children sat on the steps, Rock holding Dimple's hand and trying his best to cheer her up.

But a more doleful face than appeared at the breakfast table could not be found.

"You must get your Aunt Dora and Florence some nice flowers to take with them," said Mrs. Dallas to Dimple.

"My Aunt Dora! How queer that is, mamma. I have been wondering, is he Rock Hardy or Rock Dallas?"

"He is Rock Hardy."

"I never will get it straight," she said, as she went to get the flowers.

"Uncle Heath," she said, after she had laid the flowers in damp cotton, and put them in boxes, "you may be very happy, but I am not, and I wish you'd leave Rock with me."

He smiled as he looked down at her, and said, "I can't, dear child, but you shall see him often. Baltimore is not very far away."

"Well, I am much obliged to you for making a cousin of him," she said, as she turned away.

"Poor little girl," said he to her mother, "she takes this parting very much to heart."

"Yes," said her mother, "she has never had any very intimate friends, and her cousins have never paid her as long a visit as Florence has this time. As for Rock, he is the only boy she has ever liked at all, and he is a nice boy. You have quite a model son, Heath."

"Yes, I think so too," said he.

At last the trunks were all off, Celestine was dressed in her traveling frock, a grey veil on her hat; the children thought her very stylish.

"Poor Rubina!" sighed Dimple, bravely trying to keep back the tears.

Rock had volunteered to take charge of the two kittens, so Jet and Marble were mewing in a basket.

"And poor little Nyxy, you will be lonely too," said Dimple, hiding her face in his furry coat.

"You will be sure to write to us, won't you Dimple," said Florence, "and tell all about school, and everything."

"I will," said Dimple, choking up.

"Don't cry," said both Rock and Florence, coaxingly.

"No, I will not, I made up my mind not to, because mamma might think I didn't love her," answered Dimple, while her tears slowly trickled down her cheeks.

At last all was ready,—doll, kittens, and boxes, and the good-byes were said. Bubbles and Dimple at the gate waved handkerchiefs as long as they could see the carriage.

Then Dimple turned slowly into the house, unable to keep back the torrent of tears, and after she went into the library she buried her face in the sofa pillow, sobbing aloud; then she felt a pair of arms clasp her knees and saw two tearful black eyes looking up into her face, while Bubbles' caressing voice said, "Never min', Miss Dimple, I'se hyah."

Choose from Thousands of 1stWorldLibrary Classics By

A. M. Barnard
Ada Leverson
Adolphus William Ward
Aesop
Agatha Christie
Alexander Aaronsohn
Alexander Kielland
Alexandre Dumas
Alfred Gatty
Alfred Ollivant
Alice Duer Miller
Alice Turner Curtis
Alice Dunbar
Allen Chapman
Alleyne Ireland
Ambrose Bierce
Amelia E. Barr
Amory H. Bradford
Andrew Lang
Andrew McFarland Davis
Andy Adams
Angela Brazil
Anna Alice Chapin
Anna Sewell
Annie Besant
Annie Hamilton Donnell
Annie Payson Call
Annie Roe Carr
Annonaymous
Anton Chekhov
Archibald Lee Fletcher
Arnold Bennett
Arthur C. Benson
Arthur Conan Doyle
Arthur M. Winfield
Arthur Ransome
Arthur Schnitzler
Arthur Train
Atticus
B.H. Baden-Powell
B. M. Bower
B. C. Chatterjee
Baroness Emmuska Orczy
Baroness Orczy
Basil King
Bayard Taylor
Ben Macomber
Bertha Muzzy Bower
Bjornstjerne Bjornson

Booth Tarkington
Boyd Cable
Bram Stoker
C. Collodi
C. E. Orr
C. M. Ingleby
Carolyn Wells
Catherine Parr Traill
Charles A. Eastman
Charles Amory Beach
Charles Dickens
Charles Dudley Warner
Charles Farrar Browne
Charles Ives
Charles Kingsley
Charles Klein
Charles Hanson Towne
Charles Lathrop Pack
Charles Romyn Dake
Charles Whibley
Charles Willing Beale
Charlotte M. Braeme
Charlotte M. Yonge
Charlotte Perkins Stetson
Clair W. Hayes
Clarence Day Jr.
Clarence E. Mulford
Clemence Housman
Confucius
Coningsby Dawson
Cornelis DeWitt Wilcox
Cyril Burleigh
D. H. Lawrence
Daniel Defoe
David Garnett
Dinah Craik
Don Carlos Janes
Donald Keyhoe
Dorothy Kilner
Dougan Clark
Douglas Fairbanks
E. Nesbit
E. P. Roe
E. Phillips Oppenheim
E. S. Brooks
Earl Barnes
Edgar Rice Burroughs
Edith Van Dyne
Edith Wharton

Edward Everett Hale
Edward J. O'Biren
Edward S. Ellis
Edwin L. Arnold
Eleanor Atkins
Eleanor Hallowell Abbott
Eliot Gregory
Elizabeth Gaskell
Elizabeth McCracken
Elizabeth Von Arnim
Ellem Key
Emerson Hough
Emilie F. Carlen
Emily Bronte
Emily Dickinson
Enid Bagnold
Enilor Macartney Lane
Erasmus W. Jones
Ernie Howard Pie
Ethel May Dell
Ethel Turner
Ethel Watts Mumford
Eugene Sue
Eugenie Foa
Eugene Wood
Eustace Hale Ball
Evelyn Everett-green
Everard Cotes
F. H. Cheley
F. J. Cross
F. Marion Crawford
Fannie E. Newberry
Federick Austin Ogg
Ferdinand Ossendowski
Fergus Hume
Florence A. Kilpatrick
Fremont B. Deering
Francis Bacon
Francis Darwin
Frances Hodgson Burnett
Frances Parkinson Keyes
Frank Gee Patchin
Frank Harris
Frank Jewett Mather
Frank L. Packard
Frank V. Webster
Frederic Stewart Isham
Frederick Trevor Hill
Frederick Winslow Taylor

Friedrich Kerst
Friedrich Nietzsche
Fyodor Dostoyevsky
G.A. Henty
G.K. Chesterton
Gabrielle E. Jackson
Garrett P. Serviss
Gaston Leroux
George A. Warren
George Ade
Geroge Bernard Shaw
George Cary Eggleston
George Durston
George Ebers
George Eliot
George Gissing
George MacDonald
George Meredith
George Orwell
George Sylvester Viereck
George Tucker
George W. Cable
George Wharton James
Gertrude Atherton
Gordon Casserly
Grace E. King
Grace Gallatin
Grace Greenwood
Grant Allen
Guillermo A. Sherwell
Gulielma Zollinger
Gustav Flaubert
H. A. Cody
H. B. Irving
H.C. Bailey
H. G. Wells
H. H. Munro
H. Irving Hancock
H. R. Naylor
H. Rider Haggard
H. W. C. Davis
Haldeman Julius
Hall Caine
Hamilton Wright Mabie
Hans Christian Andersen
Harold Avery
Harold McGrath
Harriet Beecher Stowe
Harry Castlemon
Harry Coghill
Harry Houidini

Hayden Carruth
Helent Hunt Jackson
Helen Nicolay
Hendrik Conscience
Hendy David Thoreau
Henri Barbusse
Henrik Ibsen
Henry Adams
Henry Ford
Henry Frost
Henry James
Henry Jones Ford
Henry Seton Merriman
Henry W Longfellow
Herbert A. Giles
Herbert Carter
Herbert N. Casson
Herman Hesse
Hildegard G. Frey
Homer
Honore De Balzac
Horace B. Day
Horace Walpole
Horatio Alger Jr.
Howard Pyle
Howard R. Garis
Hugh Lofting
Hugh Walpole
Humphry Ward
Ian Maclaren
Inez Haynes Gillmore
Irving Bacheller
Isabel Cecilia Williams
Isabel Hornibrook
Israel Abrahams
Ivan Turgenev
J.G.Austin
J. Henri Fabre
J. M. Barrie
J. M. Walsh
J. Macdonald Oxley
J. R. Miller
J. S. Fletcher
J. S. Knowles
J. Storer Clouston
J. W. Duffield
Jack London
Jacob Abbott
James Allen
James Andrews
James Baldwin

James Branch Cabell
James DeMille
James Joyce
James Lane Allen
James Lane Allen
James Oliver Curwood
James Oppenheim
James Otis
James R. Driscoll
Jane Abbott
Jane Austen
Jane L. Stewart
Janet Aldridge
Jens Peter Jacobsen
Jerome K. Jerome
Jessie Graham Flower
John Buchan
John Burroughs
John Cournos
John F. Kennedy
John Gay
John Glasworthy
John Habberton
John Joy Bell
John Kendrick Bangs
John Milton
John Philip Sousa
John Taintor Foote
Jonas Lauritz Idemil Lie
Jonathan Swift
Joseph A. Altsheler
Joseph Carey
Joseph Conrad
Joseph E. Badger Jr
Joseph Hergesheimer
Joseph Jacobs
Jules Vernes
Julian Hawthrone
Julie A Lippmann
Justin Huntly McCarthy
Kakuzo Okakura
Karle Wilson Baker
Kate Chopin
Kenneth Grahame
Kenneth McGaffey
Kate Langley Bosher
Kate Langley Bosher
Katherine Cecil Thurston
Katherine Stokes
L. A. Abbot
L. T. Meade

L. Frank Baum
Latta Griswold
Laura Dent Crane
Laura Lee Hope
Laurence Housman
Lawrence Beasley
Leo Tolstoy
Leonid Andreyev
Lewis Carroll
Lewis Sperry Chafer
Lilian Bell
Lloyd Osbourne
Louis Hughes
Louis Joseph Vance
Louis Tracy
Louisa May Alcott
Lucy Fitch Perkins
Lucy Maud Montgomery
Luther Benson
Lydia Miller Middleton
Lyndon Orr
M. Corvus
M. H. Adams
Margaret E. Sangster
Margret Howth
Margaret Vandercook
Margaret W. Hungerford
Margret Penrose
Maria Edgeworth
Maria Thompson Daviess
Mariano Azuela
Marion Polk Angellotti
Mark Overton
Mark Twain
Mary Austin
Mary Catherine Crowley
Mary Cole
Mary Hastings Bradley
Mary Roberts Rinehart
Mary Rowlandson
M. Wollstonecraft Shelley
Maud Lindsay
Max Beerbohm
Myra Kelly
Nathaniel Hawthrone
Nicolo Machiavelli
O. F. Walton
Oscar Wilde
Owen Johnson
P.G. Wodehouse
Paul and Mabel Thorne

Paul G. Tomlinson
Paul Severing
Percy Brebner
Percy Keese Fitzhugh
Peter B. Kyne
Plato
Quincy Allen
R. Derby Holmes
R. L. Stevenson
R. S. Ball
Rabindranath Tagore
Rahul Alvares
Ralph Bonehill
Ralph Henry Barbour
Ralph Victor
Ralph Waldo Emmerson
Rene Descartes
Ray Cummings
Rex Beach
Rex E. Beach
Richard Harding Davis
Richard Jefferies
Richard Le Gallienne
Robert Barr
Robert Frost
Robert Gordon Anderson
Robert L. Drake
· Robert Lansing
Robert Lynd
Robert Michael Ballantyne
Robert W. Chambers
Rosa Nouchette Carey
Rudyard Kipling
Saint Augustine
Samuel B. Allison
Samuel Hopkins Adams
Sarah Bernhardt
Sarah C. Hallowell
Selma Lagerlof
Sherwood Anderson
Sigmund Freud
Standish O'Grady
Stanley Weyman
Stella Benson
Stella M. Francis
Stephen Crane
Stewart Edward White
Stijn Streuvels
Swami Abhedananda
Swami Parmananda
T. S. Ackland

T. S. Arthur
The Princess Der Ling
Thomas A. Janvier
Thomas A Kempis
Thomas Anderton
Thomas Bailey Aldrich
Thomas Bulfinch
Thomas De Quincey
Thomas Dixon
Thomas H. Huxley
Thomas Hardy
Thomas More
Thornton W. Burgess
U. S. Grant
Upton Sinclair
Valentine Williams
Various Authors
Vaughan Kester
Victor Appleton
Victor G. Durham
Victoria Cross
Virginia Woolf
Wadsworth Camp
Walter Camp
Walter Scott
Washington Irving
Wilbur Lawton
Wilkie Collins
Willa Cather
Willard F. Baker
William Dean Howells
William le Queux
W. Makepeace Thackeray
William W. Walter
William Shakespeare
Winston Churchill
Yei Theodora Ozaki
Yogi Ramacharaka
Young E. Allison
Zane Grey

www.ingramcontent.com/pod-product-compliance
Lightning Source LLC
Chambersburg PA
CBHW051834170626
46807CB00003B/1176